Books by Tristan Bancks

MY LiFE

& other stuFF I maDe up

Tristan Bancks

pics by
gus gordoN

RANDOM HOUSE AUSTRALIA

Tristan Bancks is an ambassador for
Room to Read. Find out more at:
www.roomtoread.org/australia

A Random House book
Published by Random House Australia Pty Ltd
Level 3, 100 Pacific Highway, North Sydney NSW 2060
www.randomhouse.com.au

First published by Random House Australia in 2011
This edition published in 2014

Addresses for companies within the Random House Group can be found at
www.randomhouse.com.au/offices

National Library of Australia
Cataloguing-in-Publication Entry

Author: Tristan Bancks
Title: My life and other stuff I made up/Tristan Bancks; illustrated by Gus Gordon
Edition: 2nd ed.
ISBN: 978 0 85798 319 0 (pbk)
Series: My life; 1.
Target Audience: Primary school age.
Other Authors/Contributors: Gordon, Gus
Dewey Number: A823.4

Cover and internal illustrations by Gus Gordon
Cover and internal design by Astred Hicks, designcherry.com
Printed in Australia by Griffin Press, an accredited ISO AS/NZS 14001:2004
Environmental Management System printer

Random House Australia uses papers that are natural, renewable and recyclable products
and made from wood grown in sustainable forests. The logging and manufacturing
processes are expected to conform to the environmental regulations of the country of
origin.

Contents

Hey.

This book is a bunch of stories I've written, ideas I've had and drawings I've done. The stories are all true. Well, they're based on stuff that's true. Sometimes I make things up. The best thing about having a book like this is that I get to be the hero — even though sometimes things kind of go wrong.

If you want to send me a message or a story or a joke or a paper plane design or other stuff you've made up, I'm at TheTomWeekly@gmail.com. Maybe I can stick it in my next book?

Anyway, hope you like it. If you don't like it, sell it on eBay. (Unless it's a library book. Librarians get kind of upset about that. Believe me.)

Tom

The Dog Kisser

My dog was licking the guy's face like it was gelato. When he was done with the nose and eyes he started in on the dude's ears.

'Attaboy,' said the guy. 'Who's my schnooky? Who's da-puppy-dog, huh? Who's da one?'

This sent Bando, my lab retriever, into a frenzy and he licked even faster. Saliva trickled down the man's face. His eyelashes hung with dog spit. His ears were glazed with goo.

I knew him

DOG dribble geL

simply as The Dog Kisser. Every day I took Bando for a walk on the beach a couple of blocks from my house and every day, no matter what time, we stumbled upon The Dog Kisser.

'C'mon, boy. C'mon, Ban,' I called, but he pretended not to hear. See, I refused to even let Bando lick my toe, let alone my face. I was a doggy love-free zone but, finally, he'd discovered somebody with no lick-limits. I couldn't watch any longer. It was wrong.

'Bando, NOW! Come!' I took him by the collar and hauled him away from the guy. 'Sorry, mate,' I said, even though I wasn't. 'We've got to go. I've got . . . stuff to do.'

I threw the chewed-up pink frisbee down the beach, towards the water. Bando bolted after it. I took one last look over my shoulder and saw Dog Kisser kneeling there on all fours in the dune. His short, dark, spiky hair was thick with dog dribble gel. He looked heartbroken as Ban scampered out of his life for another day. I shuddered and ran, finding Bando lying in the shallows, jawing on his frisbee.

That night I complained again at dinner.

'He's just being friendly,' Mum said. 'It's nice that somebody loves him. You barely go near Bando. Sometimes I wonder why we even have a dog.'

'But you haven't seen this dude go for it. It's unnatural to let a dog lick you like that.'

'Oh, don't be ridiculous,' she said. 'You're exaggerating.'

'Yet again!' said Tanya, my older sister, her only words for the entire meal.

But I wasn't exaggerating; if I'd had a tiny, button-sized video camera I'd have recorded it and put the horror show up on our new plasma while they were eating dinner. Then we'd see who was 'just being friendly'.

this was going
to be a picture
of 'tHe DoG
Kisser' snogging
my dog, but in
the end I Just
couldn't do it.

I drew
this
instead.

Next afternoon, four o'clock, after a two-minute noodle session (I was digging this prawn flavour that tasted like chicken), I put Bando on his lead and headed out the gate. I checked both ways. No sign of The Kisser. I took a right and Ban reefed the lead out of my hand, darting off to roll in a cane toad pancake on the road. Then he sprinted up the street and gobbled a browny-grey lump on the grass near the telegraph pole. Poo of some kind.

'Bando, come!' I yelled. He snaffled one last morsel and ran after me, top speed, slamming on the brakes to sniff the Give Way sign and relieve himself. At the cricket ground we cut through the sandy bush track, the fastest way to the beach. I was nervous because there was no way out if you met The Dog Kisser on the track. You could try going cross-country through the bush, but I'd done it once and been cut up pretty bad by lantana. I broke into a jog and Bando followed, overtaking me halfway up the trail.

By the time I'd caught up with him at the beach park he was giving a pit bull terrier's bottom a fairly serious inspection.

'Sorry!' I said to the owner. 'Ban, c'mon man. Gimme a break.'

I threw his mangled frisbee over the sand dune and he ran off down the path to the beach. When I arrived at the crest of the dune I scanned the beach for The DK.

Nothing.

Good.

I continued down the path and tackled Bando at the bottom, eating a face full of sand.

And then I heard it.

'Whooza bootiful one, huh?'

I wiped sand from my eyes and somehow, out of nowhere, The Dog Kisser had appeared. *Did he have some kind of underground lair down here? Was he a ghost? How did he always just show up?*

As I stood, Bando ran over and began

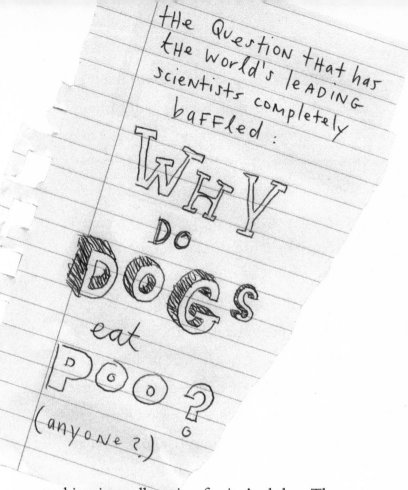

the Question that has
the world's leADING
scientists completely
baffled :

WHY
DO
DOGS
eat
POO?
(anyoNe?)

tucking in, really going for it. And then The
Dog Kisser did something I'd never seen
before. He opened his mouth and Bando
licked right inside. Everything went slo-mo
as their tongues touched. Then my mind cut
to rapid flashes of the cane toad that Ban

had rolled in, the poo he'd eaten, the pit bull terrier's bottom, then back to him pashing The DK right there on the sand. This was a new low.

'It's okay,' Dog Kisser tried to say, muffled by Bando's tongue.

'No, it's *not* okay,' I said. 'It's seriously not okay!'

I pulled Bando off the dude and he gave a high-pitched whine. Dog Kisser looked as though he was about to start blubbering too, his arms outstretched. I dragged Bando until we were a safe distance away and flung the frisbee back up the dune. Bando gave chase and I followed. I didn't look back to the Kisser. I'd made a decision. My dog-walking days were over.

For a week, Bando was in lockdown. He never left the yard. He was miserable and kept staring at me with these creepy, sad eyes. Then, one afternoon, I was watching dodgy afternoon game shows when Mum came home from work.

'Have you still not taken that dog for a walk?' she said as she dropped her bags on the dining table.

'Hi, Ma. Nice to see you, too.'

'He's dug another crater in the middle of the lawn. Say goodbye to your pocket money if you don't start walking him,' she said.

SUCH a beAutiful dAy.

Dog wAlking seRvice.

'But the –' I said.

'I know – the big, terrifying Dog Kisser's out there. Boo-hoo. Get over it. Start walking him or no allowance.'

I sat there for a minute, depressed. Then I had an idea. I jumped up and made a beeline for the pile of newspapers in the box beside the bin. I found the *Echo* and flicked to the classifieds. I knew I'd seen a dog walking service in there – a cheap one run by the church or something.

Bingo. There it was. Page 32. Salvation Army dog walking services. Three bucks an hour. I could shell out for that twice a week and still have four bucks pocket money left. I grabbed the phone and punched digits.

Next afternoon at five the doorbell rang. Bando scarpered up the hall. I came out of the lounge room, smiling, and grabbed his lead off the hallstand. I looked down towards the open front door. My jaw sagged. Kneeling on the floor, being smathered with fetid doggy love, was somebody I recognised.

'Izza puppy dog, hey. It's you, is it? Thassalovelyoneofadoggy, huh? Gunna go for walks, hey?' he said.

I could not believe it. Was I going to have to pay this guy to kiss my dog? I slowly shuffled up the hall to the open door and The DK grabbed the lead from my hand, grinning from ear to ear.

'See you in an hour!' he said, all chipper. 'C'mon, boy!'

They ran down the steps. He had seven other dogs tied up at our front gate – a sausage dog, a schnauzer, two chihuahuas, a great dane, a dalmatian and a doberman. He bent down and all eight dogs licked him from the tips of his fingers to the top of his head. Saliva flew everywhere, showering our front path and, just for a second, I felt jealous. Those dogs loved him. It didn't feel like anybody loved me as much as they loved him. Not my mum, my sister. Nobody. I suddenly felt cold and alone. And yet here he was, a lowly dog kisser, being adored by hounds of every shape, colour and breed.

Without thinking I started walking down the steps. I didn't really know what I was doing but something was drawing me towards them. A second or two later I kneeled on the path and Bando and a couple of other dogs bounded over and started licking me. Their pink tongues tickled my ears and nose. At first I pulled away but, I had to admit, it kind of felt good. And with each coat of saliva on my neck and face I felt more loved. I felt like one of them, like part of the pack. And, in that moment, my life had changed forever. I'd crossed the line. I, Tom Weekly, was a dog kisser.

Survey: Percentage of People Who Like Being Licked by Dogs

Jack reckons I'm weird because I let Bando lick me now, so I asked everyone in my class if they're dog kissers or not. Here's what they said:

Dog Kissers: 67%

Not Dog Kissers: 25%

Undecided: 8%

So, maybe the non-dog-kissers are the freaks?

Hot Dog Eat

'Beat Mad Dog. Whatever it takes. Do it for me. Do it for the family.'

These were my pop's dying words as he handed me a small, flat, brown jar of paste. He pressed it into my palm and closed my fingers around it. I knew exactly what was inside. I held his hand. I had no idea how I was going to pull this off.

The sign across the front of the grand white tent read, 'Fast Eddie's 27th Annual Dog Eat'. Groups of people drifted across the grassy

Where Are all tHe hot DOGs going to fit?

beachfront park towards the tent, all hoping to get a seat for the biggest event of the year.

I ran my finger over the jar in my pocket, walked into the tent and up three steps onto the stage. Half the competitors were already seated at the long row of tables covered in clean, white tablecloths. The people in the crowd were sweating and fanning themselves with their programs. There wasn't a breath of breeze. I took my seat, looking down at the audience. Behind them, through the back of the tent, I could see blue sky and ocean. On the table in front of me there were six or seven tall paper cups filled with water for dipping hot dog buns into. It made them easier to swallow. There were 12 volunteers in yellow T-shirts in front of the stage. They were ready to plate up the dogs and keep count of how many each competitor had eaten.

A couple of little kids in the crowd pointed at me and laughed. I didn't blame them. I looked across at the other contestants. I was the youngest and skinniest on the stage. I looked nothing like a champion dog eater. But then Pop had been wiry, too, and he was almost a legend.

'Hey, Tom.'

I looked down in front of the stage. It was Jack, my best friend, in among all the volunteers.

'Stilton's been taking bets all morning,'

he said. 'You're a 200 to one shot. I just put a dollar on you. That means I get 200 bucks if you win.'

'A dollar?' I said. 'Aren't I worth more than that?'

'You're at 200 to one. I'm probably the only person who *has* put a dollar on you.'

The crowd suddenly went wild. The stage shook violently. I turned and quickly realised that this was no earthquake. It was Mad Dog Morgan. Red beard. Blue overalls. Bushy eyebrows, like small brush fires above his eyes.

He stopped, looked out at the audience and shoved his gigantic fist into his mouth. He shook his head from side to side like a dog with a bone. The audience went nuts. A bunch of guys in the front row tried to jam their fists into their mouths, too. It felt like we were at a wrestling match.

Last year Mad Dog punched out 56 dogs in ten minutes, beating his own record. My

Mad Dog Morgan and me.

grrrrrrr.

gulp.

grandad did 54. Pop had come second place
every year for 26 years, since the competition
began. Mad Dog was just 13 dogs shy of the
world title, and he was telling everybody that
this was his year. Pop had been thinking that it
was *his* year, too. Right up until he died.

Mad Dog sat down next to me, casting
a long shadow. It was like the sun had gone

behind a cloud. The metal legs of the chair strained under his weight. Someone rushed in from behind and squeezed a second chair under his other enormous butt cheek.

He looked across at me and started to laugh. Then he began to howl. He opened his mouth wide and threw back his head. Stalactites of spit hung from his top lip.

'You!' he said. Then he laughed some more. 'He sent you! Bahahahahaha . . .'

A chant went up from the crowd: 'Mad Dog, Mad Dog, he's our man. If he can't eat it, no one can!' Mad Dog thrust both fists into the air and his supporters went mental. I looked at him – his nine unshaven chins, the fat hanging down from his forehead almost covering his eyes, those fiery red brows. I listened to his heavy breathing. It was like a vacuum cleaner with a golf ball stuck in the tube. The guy was a physical mess. But today, one day a year, Mad Dog was royalty in this town. Could I really take that away from him? Didn't a guy like him deserve a single day of glory out of 365?

'Win!' I heard a raspy voice say.

I looked over my shoulder. Standing behind me, leaning close to my ear, was the ghostly figure of my pop. I wasn't scared of him. I felt calm, but his eyes looked desperate, like he needed this badly. So he could rest in peace.

'Okay,' I whispered.

His image faded. I looked around and he was gone.

I had to win this thing. For him. No choice. No mercy. I felt in my pocket for the jar. I took it out and looked at it, keeping it below table-level. I turned it over in my fingers. I had to admit, I was still worried that the paste might have had something to do with Pop dying. He had been out in his back shed for months, just him and the cat. He stirred and mixed all day, trying millions of weird and wacky ingredients for his magical paste, something that would give him the edge in the Dog Eat. Then, one day, about a month ago, he called me. 'I've done it,' he said in an excited whisper. 'It's perfect. It's called BLAM.'

I hadn't even tried the paste yet. I wanted to when I was training but I was too scared. I pushed the jar back into my pocket. I looked along the row of 11 losers who had turned out to compete. Surely I could beat these guys. *Maybe I could win this without the paste?* I thought. *If I just put my mind to it.*

'Ladies annnnnd gentlemen,' said a commanding voice. Everybody turned to the left-hand end of the table where Eddie Holmes, founder of the comp and owner of Fast Eddie's Dogs, had picked up the microphone. 'Welcome to Fast Eddie's Famous Dog Eat on the beachfront, right here in Kings Bay.'

People cheered and fanned themselves madly.

'I know it's hot in here but I believe we're in for a real treat.'

The crowd was alive, buzzing.

'Who here thinks Australia's very own, *our* very own Maaaad Dog Morgan has what it takes to beat the world record – 68 dogs in ten minutes – set at Coney Island, New York?'

'Whooooooooo!' Whistling and screaming. People going nuts, standing up, fists in their mouths, shaking their heads.

'Good, good. And who thinks our other contenders here have a chance?' he asked.

'*Boo!*' A few kids in the second row threw their screwed-up programs. One of them hit me in the forehead.

'Okay,' Holmes said, pleased with the reaction. 'Let's get this dog-fest started. Our contestants look hunnnnnngry!'

The loudest cheer yet. The crowd were like animals.

'Audience ready?'

They roared.

'Dog eaters ready?'

Screams and howls.

'Let's eat!' He rang the famous Fast Eddie's Dog Eat bell and we were away.

The volunteers placed plates piled high with hot dogs in front of each of us.

I jumped to my feet. I was the only challenger to stand, but this was one of my secret weapons to help the dogs go down easier. I grabbed a dog, snapped it in half and jammed both ends into my open mouth. As I chewed I took a bun, dipped it in water, swallowed the dogs in lumps then 'drank' the bun, just like Pop used to. I reached for more dogs.

We were only 20 seconds into the competition. I was trying to stay calm, not get panicky. I glanced across at Mad Dog.

'Morgan reaches for dog number four,' Fast Eddie called.

I jammed dog two in and barked it down with a big gulp of water. I would have preferred butter, sauce and mustard, but Pop always said that those things made you sick after 40 or 50 hot dogs.

As I shoved in dog three the commentator screamed, 'Nummmber six for Maaaaaad Dooooooog.'

He was already three dogs ahead.

I jumped and moved around, helping the dogs go down, but Mad Dog just sat there. The only things moving were his jaw and his dog hand.

'Threeee minutes,' was the call on the mic. 'It's like ballet watching these contestants eat, isn't it folks?'

As I wolfed another bun I turned to see half a frankfurt falling from Mad Dog's mouth and a squished bun slopping around in his jaws. There's no way ballet could be this gross.

I grabbed dogs 23 and 24. I snapped them, jammed them in together, chewed twice and slammed them down with a soggy double-bun chaser. I was struggling. I looked out into the crowd and saw my mum standing at the back of the tent. Nan was sitting in front of her. They both looked nervous. Mum hadn't wanted me to enter the competition at all, but now she had this look on her face like it really mattered to her that I won. She gripped her hands together under her chin, like she was praying for me to do this for her dad. Nan covered her eyes. Maybe I reminded her too much of Pop?

'Thirty-two dogs in five minutes for Maaaaaad Doooooooggggggggg. He's on target for the world title!' Fast Eddie called. I was only on dog 25. I was dropping further behind by the second and the dogs weren't sitting right in my belly. I'd been watching this competition for enough years to know that seven dogs was an almost unbeatable lead.

'What are you doing?' my grandfather said.

I nearly choked. I turned to my left and there was Pop, leaning over my shoulder again.

'This was my dying wish, you nincompoop,' he said. 'Use the BLAM! I didn't spend a year inventing it just to watch you throw the competition away!'

I stopped chewing.

He disappeared.

I reached into my pocket. The jar felt cool. I looked up towards Fast Eddie. There was a Dog Eat official standing next to him, watching us carefully. *Was BLAM performance-enhancing paste?* I wondered. *If I got caught for cheating, wouldn't that be worse than if I lost fair and square?*

'Nincompoop,' I heard again, so I dipped two buns in water with my free hand and jammed them into my gob. With my other hand I untwisted the cap on the jar, still in my pocket, and dug my finger into the moist paste. As soon as the buns went down my throat I ate the scoop of BLAM, then snapped and stuffed a two-dog chaser in.

At first nothing happened – it just tasted like hot dog – but when the BLAM hit the back of my throat the flavour washed over me. It was the most disgusting thing I'd ever tasted. Everything in my mouth and stomach fizzed all of a sudden, like a shook-up bottle of lemonade. Then, a few seconds later, my whole body went cold. Goosebumps everywhere. Meanwhile I stuffed two more soggy buns into my mouth. My arms and legs were freezing. My heart was beating like bongos.

Then BLAM!

Everything went hot and I started sweating. I took a big slug of water and snapped and jammed two more dogs in.

That was when the amazing thing happened. The dogs just seemed to turn to water when they hit my throat. They went down so easily. I inhaled the bun chaser. All of a sudden I was knocking off dogs and buns at twice my regular speed. My body was still on fire but I was a dog eating machine.

a hot Dog eAting MAcHiNe

I was drinking them down like hot dog milkshakes. They were delicious.

'Forty-seven dogs!' Eddie Holmes called at the seven-minute mark. 'Mad Dog's on track to make world history right here, today.'

Then the volunteer serving my dogs called out 'This kid's done 44!'

'We have a competition on our hands! The skinny kid in the middle on 44 dogs is the grandson of Cliff Weekly, everybody.'

The crowd cheered, nowhere near as loudly as they did for Mad Dog, but it still felt good. Pop had been loved in this competition and lots of people felt he should have won three years back, but he was robbed on a technicality. He hadn't renewed his membership to the International Federation of Competitive Eating, so they stripped him of his crown.

A chant went up. 'Go Weekly. Go Weekly. Go!'

I felt Mad Dog turn to look at me as his mouth harvested two whole dogs, buns and all. But I didn't care. Having the crowd behind me made me lift my pace even more. Whatever BLAM was, it had turned my mouth into a food processor. I was a weapon of mass digestion. At the nine-minute mark Mad Dog and I were neck and neck on 62 dogs.

'This is one dog-eat-dog competition!' Fast Eddie howled.

With 30 seconds to go it was all locked up at 65 dogs. I needed to chow down four in half a minute to break the world record, so I threw them back like they were French fries. I knew that BLAM would take care of them.

But my body was starting to revolt. I felt like I had dogs right up to my throat, jammed in around my heart and lungs, filling up every spare space inside. My stomach felt as though it was ready to rip open. They were out to my

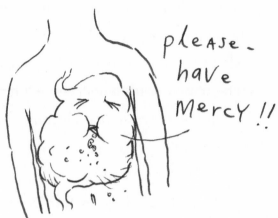

please-
have
Mercy !!

shoulders
and starting to
creep into my legs, too.

Mad Dog was groaning and sweating real
bad, keeping one eye on me. He burped a
repulsive, hot-doggy burp. I had 15 seconds
to eat three dogs and my body started to
convulse. It was giving up. Even with BLAM I
had nowhere to jam more dogs.

I pushed one more in and somehow
managed to get it down, taking me to 67 dogs.
Before I could get to 68, Fast Eddie's bell
rang, heralding the end of the competition.
I covered my face. I was one dog shy of

equalling the world record, two dogs shy of beating it. Pop was right. I was a nincompoop. Mad Dog did another real bad hot dog burp. The stench nearly knocked me off my chair. Then the crowd started chanting, 'Tom, Tom, Tom, Tom!'

I looked up slowly.

'Sixty-seven dogs for Tom Weekly,' Eddie Holmes called. 'Sixty-six dogs for Morgan! We have a new cham-pion!'

The crowd went crazy for me. I wanted to smile but all I could do was groan and try to swallow the last bit of doughy bun in my mouth. Then I saw the woman who had been counting how many dogs Mad Dog ate. She was tall and blonde, wearing a yellow volunteer's T-shirt. She rushed over to Fast Eddie and whispered something in his ear. She was looking my way. Eddie Holmes looked down the row of dog eaters, frowning.

He walked across the stage and stopped

next to me. I
looked at him.
He leaned in
and whispered
something
to me. My
head dropped.

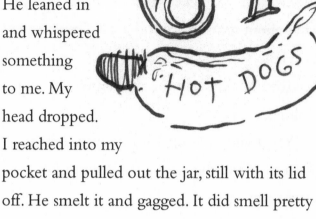

I reached into my
pocket and pulled out the jar, still with its lid
off. He smelt it and gagged. It did smell pretty
bad.

'What is this?' he asked.

All I could say was, 'BLAM!'

That night I sat by myself at the dining table.
Mum was up in town getting a DVD and
chocolate to make me feel better. My sister
was in her room. I was trying to eat a lettuce
leaf. Pop always said to eat water-rich foods
after a competition to help digestion. I could

taste BLAM in my throat. I still couldn't put my finger on what it tasted like, though. The phone rang. I panicked. I let it ring. And ring. After about six rings I hit the 'talk' button.

'Hello.'

'Tom Weekly,' said the deep voice of Eddie Holmes.

'Yes,' I said, waiting. I was prepared for the worst. I'd done the wrong thing and I knew I had to pay for it.

'We have had the paste tested.'

I hung my head. I'd been dreading this all afternoon.

'It checked out okay,' he said.

'Really?' I straightened in my chair.

'Really. Which means you stole Mad Dog's crown. Congratulations. You'll be on the front page of tomorrow's paper.'

I felt Pop leaning over my left shoulder again. I could see his reflection in the back window of the house and he was happy. He was very happy. Twenty-six years he'd been working for this, and I had brought it home. Then he was gone again. That was the last time I saw my grandfather.

'That is so good. Thank you!' I said.

'There was something that I wanted to talk to you about, though, son,' Eddie said.

'Yes, sir.'

'This BLAM. I don't think you should eat any more of it.'

'What do you mean?' I said. BLAM was the reason I'd won. I figured that if I ate some at the *beginning* of next year's competition, rather than halfway through, I could take out the world title, easy.

'It has some very odd ingredients,' Eddie said.

'What?' I asked.

'Well, they're legal. There's nothing in the rules that says you can't eat them, but I just don't know that you would *want* to eat them.'

'What?' I asked, a little scared, knowing that Pop had been experimenting with some pretty weird stuff.

'Your grandfather didn't tell you?'

'No,' I said.

'Well,' began Holmes, 'the paste is made up of three key ingredients. One is green grass.'

'Yeah.'

'There's lemonade . . .'

'That's not too bad,' I said, sort of tasting the grassy, lemony flavour in my mouth.

'It's the last ingredient that's a bit strange,' he said.

'What is it? No, let me guess. Is it cauliflower? Or cabbage? That's what it sort of tastes like.'

'No,' he said. 'No, it's neither of those.'

'Is it fish? It sort of maybe tastes a bit fishy.'

'Well,' he said, 'yes, I would say there's probably fish *in* it, but –'

'I give up,' I said. 'What is it?'

There was silence on the line for a moment. He cleared his throat. 'It was a small amount of vomit. Cat vomit, we think.'

I screamed in his ear. Then I started choking.

'Tom?' he said.

My body jerked. I scratched at my tongue, trying to scrape the BLAM off. Then I dropped the phone.

'Tom?' I heard as I ran. 'Tom?'

But I was gone. I bolted to the bathroom, and I don't even want to tell you what happened when I got there.

It's been a few days now since the competition. We've been over at Nan and Pop's, helping Nan pack some of Pop's stuff into boxes. I keep asking myself the same questions over and over: Knowing the ingredients in that paste, will I do it again next year? Will I eat BLAM and go for the world title? Will I do it for my pop?

It makes me physically sick to say it . . . but I think I will.

Would you?

Facts on Joey 'Jaws' Chestnut, World Champion Eater

Joey Chestnut is a world-famous competitive eater. Here are some of his records:

68 hot dogs in 10 minutes

103 hamburgers in 8 minutes

4.5 litres of milk in 41 seconds

4.5 kilograms of pork in 12 minutes

(that's the weight of 1.5 chihuahuas)

37 slices of pizza in 10 minutes

More about Joey Jaws:

http://en.wikipedia.org/wiki/Joey_Chestnut

Weirdest Stuff I've Ever Eaten

- Ants (On holidays in Alice Springs)

- Crocodile (Tastes like chewy fish)

- Goanna (Stringy — a bit like lamb)

- Red-hot chilli pepper (Lost a bet with Jack — pretended it didn't bother me at all)

- Chicken feet (Heaps of bones)
- Sea slugs (Pretty wrong)
- Pig's stomach (With Filipino friends)
- Playdough
- Dirt
- A fly (That one was an accident)

Teleporter

'What're you doing, Freak?' Jack asks, coming in through our back door.

I flick open the window flap of the large cardboard box that I'm sitting in. The box is in the middle of the lounge room floor.

'It's a teleporter,' I say, letting the flap close again.

'It looks like a cardboard box covered in foil.' He lifts the flap and stares in at me. He's holding a soccer ball.

'The reflective coating is actually a heat shield to protect the machine as it zings through space,' I explain.

'Yeah, right.' Jack snorts as he runs his eye over the ingenious machine that I've spent all morning on. 'How's it work?'

'Well, you type in where you want to go and you disappear, reappearing in that place.'

He looks at me. 'I know what a *teleporter* does, but this is a *cardboard box*. I want to know how a *box* does that.'

'Whatever.' I pull a string, closing the cardboard flap, locking him out. I prepare for teleportation. He'll see who the freak is when I disappear.

Jack lifts the flap again to find me punching letters into the keypad.

'What are you doing?'

'Inputting my destination,' I say. I click the intercom button. 'Teleportation to commence in T minus three minutes.'

'So you're telling me you can type a location into a keypad drawn on a box in orange texta and then the box –'

'The teleporter,' I say.

'The *teleporter,*' he says, 'will take you there.'

'Correctamundo. But you've got to believe.'

'As if.'

'You coming?' I ask. 'We can go somewhere where there's food if you like. They reckon there are awesome pizza pies in Chicago. And in Bavaria they have Black Forest cake.'

Jack doesn't look too happy but he pulls open the door and gets in.

'You should be more thankful to someone who's taking you to Bavaria,' I say.

'I just want to play soccer.'

My eyes light up. 'Where? London? Wembley Stadium?'

'Bonehead.'

I tap 'Wembley Stadium' into the keypad. 'Please fasten seatbelts, ensure seatbacks are in the upright position and tray tables are stowed away.'

'Get on with it!' he says.

'Please arm doors and cross-check,' I say quietly.

Jack shoots me a look.

'Ten ... nine ... eight ... seven ...'

He shakes his head. 'This is baby stuff, man. If anyone from school saw us doing this ...'

' ... three ... two ... one ...' Then I make these awesome noises like an explosion and something flinging through the air at the speed of light. My sound effects are so real that I can actually feel the heat and electricity of teleportation as we make our maiden voyage.

'I reckon this is how Thomas Edison felt when he made the first phone call,' I say to Jack in a loud voice. 'And how Doc from *Back to the Future* felt when he invented the time machine.'

Suddenly there's silence. I wait, listening.

'Are we there yet?' Jack asks.

'You check.'

Jack opens the door and steps out, taking in the surroundings. I step out after him. I'm amazed. 'Pretty cool, huh?'

'No,' Jack says. 'It's not cool. It's your lounge room.'

'Can't you see the crowd?'

Back to the Present

He looks around. 'I can see a really ugly painting of a horse that your mum did.'

'But what about the lights?' I tilt my face up, closing my eyes, grinning, bathing in the golden glow of a Wembley night game.

'Australia versus England. Half-time's over,' I say, eyes still closed. 'It's all locked up at 1–1. World Cup match. Crowd going nuts, chanting in the stands. You can feel the English winter on your skin. Your nose is red and running a bit. Your jersey's sticking to your body, damp from the fog enshrouding the field.'

'Enshrouding?' Jack says.

'Your toes are numb in your boots from the icy dew on the field.'

I open one eye and notice that Jack's got his eyes closed, and he's wiggling his toes a little. He rubs the skin on his arms.

'It does feel a little cool,' he says.

'The fans are heaps crazier than an Aussie crowd. They live in England so soccer's the only thing they've got to live for. The whistle goes.'

I open my other eye and grab Jack's ball out of his hands, drop it onto my right foot and pass it to him. He flicks it back to me. I move up-field. 'Players are closing in, left and right. I'm in all sorts of trouble.'

'Gimme the ball,' Jack says.

I fire it across. He dodges around one defender, the coffee table, and then past the teleporter.

'The crowd are booing,' I say. 'There'll be a riot if the Aussies score this early in the second half. If we win, England is out of the World Cup, beaten by convicts. Tonight, though, you're unstoppable, Jack Danalis. You're on fire.'

'I'm on fire!' he says, getting serious.

'The young hot shot is on his first outing with the Australian team. The kid with the golden boots. He's toying with the ball, like he's got it on a string. What's he gonna do? He dodges left, then right.'

I can tell Jack's getting into it now. 'He can feel the crowd, the lights, the pressure.

A nation's hopes and dreams rest on this kid's shoulders. Pass!' I yell, but Jack, psyched up, decides to shoot. He kicks the ball as hard as he can. I stop and watch it rise off the boot, flying through the air like a small black-and-white missile. It looks beautiful up there, spinning around and around.

'It's got to be a goal. This thing can't miss,' I scream.

But I quickly realise that there is no goal. We're not at Wembley Stadium. This is my lounge room, and the ball is either going to smash the window or the TV. Jack screams, 'Noooooooooooooo!' and covers his face with his hands.

SLAM! It hits the new plasma. The flatscreen wobbles on its small, black stand, rocking back, then forward, teetering on the edge of the cabinet. I want to run and catch it but my feet are solid concrete. I stand and stare, mouth open, as it finally tips forward, plunging to the floor, ripping the wiring out of the wall. There's a BANG, a small shower of orange sparks, a sharp white light, an electrical fizzing sound. The screen is face down on the floor.

I look to Jack. He's still holding his head in his hands. I can hear cicadas, a truck reversing, the bark of a dog.

I groan in pain.

'Did that just happen?' Jack asks.

'Yes,' I say. 'It just happened.'

'This is your fault,' Jack says.

'What?'

'You got me all fired up. "Wembley Stadium"? "Young hot shot"? "Golden boots"? "Ball on a string"? You did this,' he says, pointing a finger at me. But I can tell by his eyes that he's scared. He knows my mum will lose it, big time. This is worse than when he hit a cricket ball into the garden and smashed Buddha's head off. It's worse than the

time a magic trick went wrong and he spilt
red ink all over Mum's rug.

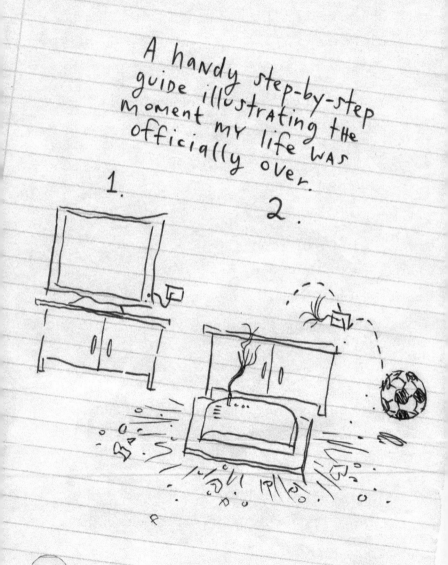

A handy step-by-step
guide illustrating the
moment my life was
officially over.

1.

2.

At that moment I hear the most terrible sound in the whole world – Mum's car driving up our street. It's still maybe a couple of hundred metres away, but I know her gear changes. At Christmas time I trained myself to know when she was approaching so that I could snoop for presents.

The engine growls.

'Oh no.'

'Let's hide it,' Jack says.

'It's like the centrepiece of the whole room. And it's new. She'll know.'

'Well, flip it over. Let's have a look. Maybe it's not too bad.'

We grab an edge of the screen each and lift.

We stare.

The cracks are like a giant spider web, filling the screen.

My mum's car pulls into the driveway.

I want to cry.

We rest the corpse of the TV back on the floor.

'Let's go,' Jack says.

'Where to? Out back?'

'No.' Jack climbs into the teleporter. 'New York, Egypt, Jamaica – wherever, dude.'

I stand outside the box, looking at him through the cardboard window flap. My mum's car door slams.

'It's a box covered in foil!'

My mother walks along the front path.

'I know that,' he says, 'but it's also a teleporter. The reflective coating is a heat shield to protect the machine as it zings through space. That's what you said.' He's getting desperate now.

My mum's key hits the front door lock.

'No it's not,' I say. 'It's a box. Let's go. Out the back. Now.'

'You gotta believe.'

The front door opens.

'Hello-o, I'm ho-ome,' Mum says from the hall.

I want to run but what am I supposed to do? I can't believe Jack is doing this. Is he insane? If I try to run out back now she'll see me for sure. There's only one thing to do.

I dive into the teleporter and start punching letters on the keypad.

'Where're we going?' Jack asks.

'Anywhere that's safer than here,' I say. 'Afghanistan, maybe.'

'Oh. My. Goodness,' says Mum from the

lounge room doorway. I can imagine her standing there, mouth open. I know what's coming.

'Tom!' she screams.

'Ten, nine, eight, seven, six . . .' Jack whispers quickly.

'Tom!'

I'm not coming back for a long, long time.

'Five, four, three, two, one.'

'T-o-o-o-o-o-o-o-o-o-o-o-o-o-o-o-o-o-m!'

Annoying Things That Jack Does to Make People Not Like Him

* Stands too close to people and, in a high-pitched, annoying voice, asks them lots of questions about their pets. (Especially if they don't have any.)

* Slaps someone on the arm. Then offers to kiss it better.
* Asks someone to pick a colour between 1 and 100.
* Asks someone to pick a kind of flower between 100 and 2.

HAVE YOU SEEN THIS PERSON?

STAY WELL CLEAR – he is <u>VERY</u> ANNOYING! ANSWERS to tHe name of 'Jack'

* When it starts raining, he looks up at the drops and starts screaming 'I'm melting, I'm melting!' Then he falls on the ground and swims like a frog.

* Sometimes he barks really loudly and angrily at people for no reason.

* He once gave his dog a nice, juicy steak. Then took it off her.

* When he had nits, he went in when his little sister was sleeping and rubbed his hair on hers.

Top Ten Nit Cures

I randomly asked kids in the playground for the weirdest nit cures their parents had used on them. Here's the top ten:

1. Wasabi
2. Mayonnaise
3. Truck wash
4. Peanut butter
5. Kerosene
6. Orange juice
7. Dog shampoo
8. Ice-cream
9. Honey
10. Frontline (The dog flea treatment)

My Nan's Tougher

WARNING: Adults should not read
this story under any circumstances.

'My nan's tougher than yours.'

'No she's not.'

'Yes she is.'

Whenever we walk home from school Jack
always goes on about how tough his nan is.
I'm sick of it.

'My nan's so tough,' he says, 'she bakes big
chunks of glass into her cookies rather than
choc chips. When she chews them you can
hear the glass crunching in her teeth.'

I climb up on to the sandstone fence that
runs around the park in the middle of town. I
balance like a tightrope walker. 'Well, my nan's
so tough that when I arrive at her place she
hugs me and my guts nearly squeeze out of
my eyeballs.'

'My nan has this motorised rocking chair,'
Jack says, looking up at me. 'It rocks back and
forth twice as fast as a normal one. It rocks
so fast that her head smashes against the chair
thousands of times a day, and she thinks it's a
nice head massage.'

'The other day me and my nan had a
cherry-spitting contest, and she spat the seeds
so far that the New Zealand Prime Minister
made a formal complaint,' I tell him. I jump
down off the fence and continue on up the
main street towards the shops.

'My nan's so tough she's a cat-burglar.
She steals people's cats, brings them back to
the nursing home and makes cat soup out

of them. She tells the other inmates that it's chicken.'

'My nan's teeth are so dirty she has to use a toilet brush to clean them,' I say.

'My nan's breath smells like a warm tuna smoothie,' Jack fires back.

'My nan uses sandpaper instead of toilet paper.'

'Mine uses her hand.'

'My nan plants weeds in her front garden and sprays the flowers with poison.'

'We gave my nan chrysanthemums on Mother's Day – and she ate them.'

'Mine knits chain-mail jumpers.'

'Mine gave up knitting to pursue her other interest – kickboxing.'

'My nan has a Great Dane as big as a horse,' I say. 'Its poo is bigger than an elephant's.'

'My nan's dog has two mouths: one at the front of its head and one at the back. If you pat its neck it bites you with its back-mouth.'

'The fruitcake
my nan makes is so full of dog
fur,' I say, 'that it's like eating an actual dog.'

'Mine rolls her lamingtons in maggots
rather than coconut.'

'My nan's –'

'Alright!' Jack snaps, stopping and turning
to me. 'If your nan's so tough, I dare her to
fight my nan.'

'What?' I laugh.

'I'm serious.'

He really is serious. I laugh again, nervously this time.

'Well?' he says.

'Um. Well . . .'

'Chicken,' he says.

'What?'

'I said you're chicken.'

'Don't call me chicken. Name the place – my nan'll be there and she'll mash your nan like a potato.'

'Saturday. 6 am. In the alley down near my nan's nursing home.'

'Deal,' I say.

'Make sure she's there.'

'She'll be there.'

'Good.'

'Good.'

Saturday, 5.54 am. I ride up to the mouth of the alleyway. It runs off the main street, down near the industrial estate. It's pretty dark and grimy. Brown brick walls run all the way to a dead end, where there's a door. I think it's the back of the old spaghetti factory. Bottles and rubbish lie everywhere.

'You came,' says a voice.

I peer through the semi-darkness. Jack is sitting, legs hanging over the edge of a dirty green dumpster about halfway down the alley.

'Thought you wouldn't show,' he says.

'And miss out on the greatest day of my life?'

Jack burps. He jumps down and walks to the opening of the alley to meet me.

'Here she comes,' he says.

I listen. There is a tiny *hum-buzzing*. It seems to be coming closer.

'Does she drive a granny cart?' I ask.

Jack doesn't say anything. I've never met Jack's nan, but if she has to ride a motorised cart around the corner from the nursing home it must mean she's really frail. Maybe he's been lying about her the whole time. I'm going to feel terrible if my nan beats up a woman who can't even walk.

I hear a faint *click-clack, click-clack* coming from the other end of the street. I'd know that sound anywhere. My nan's walking frame. Two of the rubber feet are missing so it always makes this *click-clack* of metal on tar.

The *hum-buzz* gets much louder as the granny cart rounds a nearby corner onto the main street. My jaw hangs open. This is not like any granny cart I've ever seen. It's hot pink. The wheels are like monster-truck wheels. The numberplate reads, 'SUE'. Jack's nan is sitting about two metres above the road in this hotted-up beast. There's a screech of rubber on tar as the cart pulls up on the footpath next to us. The engine cuts. The wheel rims have little silver skulls around the edge. I look up at Jack's nan. She is not frail. She is very not frail.

Click-clack, click-clack.

I give Jack a frown that says, *Why didn't you tell me?*

He grins and shrugs his shoulders.

Jack's nan is the largest woman I have ever seen outside the *Guinness Book of Records*. She is like a wrecking ball designed to bring down skyscrapers. You know those American people you see on the news who haven't left their bed in ten years and need the roof to be removed from their house so that a crane can lift them into an ambulance? Well, she's not quite that big, but I reckon she's about ten of me stuck together.

Click-clack, click-clack.

I turn. My nan is about 30 metres away, coming past the motor wrecker's gate. Her white poodle, Ponka, is on a red lead at her side. I want to bolt down the street and tell Nan to run for her life, to head for the hills, that this woman will peel her like a banana.

I hear the suspension on the cart squeak loudly as Jack's nan clambers down. An overweight black-and-white dog drops off the cart after her. It pants loudly like it has something caught in its throat. I try to see if it has an extra mouth on its neck, but I don't want to get too close.

My nan comes to a stop and the street is silent.

'Hi, Nan.' I give her a kiss on her soft cheek.

'Hello, Love,' she says. 'Is this the lady who wants to punch my lights out?'

'Yeah, this is her.'

'Lovely to meet you,' she says.

Nan's not wearing her glasses. She squints. I can tell that she can't see Jack's nan at all. They stand about five metres apart at the opening of the alley, each with a dog at their side.

In the blue corner: my nan, Nancy, 75-years old, hunched over her walking frame, light blue shirt with dark blue flowers and a knee-length dress. Lipstick on her teeth, clutching a large handbag. She is a frail biscuit of a woman. In the red corner: Jack's nan, Sue, maybe 65, wearing a yellow shirt the size of a two-man tent and a pair of jeans. Dark brown hair tied in a bun. Gold rope chain around her neck like a rapper. A tattoo of a lizard on her arm. She grins, showing a wide, black slot where her front teeth once were.

Jack and I look at each other. Can we really make these women fight? Aren't there laws against this? Or is that just roosters?

'You ready?' Jack says.

'Um.'

'You ready, Nanna?' Jack asks.

Jack's nan spits on the ground in front of her. 'Let's do this.'

'Can you give me a minute?' I say to Jack, taking my nan aside, walking her into the alley. 'You don't have to do this. I didn't know that –'

'No. In my day if you said you were going
to do something, you did it. Now where is
she?'

'You need your glasses,' I tell her.

'No I do not. They're at home. They pinch
me behind the ears.'

'There are things you should know about
Jack's grandma.'

'Don't try to talk me out of this, Thomas.'

'But she's –'

JAck's
nan

'Don't you worry,' she says, parking her walking frame against the green dumpster. 'I'm looking forward to this. I haven't had a good catfight since I was in Fifth Form.'

She turns and puts up her dooks, old-skool style. She rotates her fists in circles in front of her.

Sue laughs. 'This'll be good,' she mumbles, waddling into the alley. She turns her head to the right and then to the left. It pops like bubble wrap being twisted. She strides forward and I swear I feel the ground quake.

My heart is banging. What will I tell Mum if Nan gets a black eye? Or worse.

'Okay, ladies,' Jack says in his best referee's voice. 'Two-minute rounds. Best of three. May the best nan win.'

Round One

For the first minute they just circle each other. The clock ticks down. My nan twists her head slightly, straining to hear where Sue is because she can't see her.

'Come on, you!' Nan says. 'Let's dance.'

Jack's nan smiles, waits, then runs at my nan. Well, not exactly *runs*. It's more of a slow-motion bounding, like a hairy mammoth in a stampede. My nan seems totally unaware that she's about to be cleaned up.

'STOOOOOPPPPP!' I shout, but it's too late. Jack's nan leaps off one foot and dives through the air.

'Where are you?' my nan calls out. 'You can

run but you can't –'

BAM! Sue nails her. The two women hit the footpath, hard. Nan disappears beneath Sue. She's been Flat Stanleyed, turned into a pancake. Rather than walking through doors, she'll be able to slip under them from now on. When she goes on holidays, we'll post her rather than send her on a plane.

Even Jack looks worried. I want to go and roll Sue

my Flat NAN

off, but I'm scared of what I'll find. I don't want a rice cracker for a grandmother.

Then I hear, 'Get off me or I'll sock you one in the kisser.'

I'm so relieved to hear Nan's voice. Sue rolls aside and my nan emerges. She gives Sue a kick in the knee. 'You try that again, you Heffalump, and I'll give you the ol' Nancy Weekly one-two.'

I race over. 'Are you alright?'

Her hair looks crazy, her lipstick is smeared all over one cheek and her dress is torn – but she seems okay.

'*Ding-ding*,' says Jack. 'That's two minutes. End of round one.'

'Let's just stop this now,' I say to Nan as she heads back to the corner where her walking frame sits.

'*Why?*' she asks.

'Why? Because you nearly died about ten seconds ago.'

'Oh, don't exaggerate. That's the problem with you kids. You make mountains out of molehills.'

'We don't. You just –'

'When's round two?' she says, squinting into the distance.

Round Two

The next round goes just as badly as the first. Sue pulls out every lowdown, old-lady trick in the book. She rubs a tube of cream for crusty feet into my nan's eyes. Nan squeals loudly. She rips off my nan's wig and throws it into the dumpster. I didn't even know Nan wore a wig.

Sue grabs a cookbook out of the back of her cart, a thick one by Margaret somebody, and thumps my nan over the head. She whips a pair of knitting needles out of the back of her jeans and jabs Nan all over.

Nan says, '*Ooo,*' every time she gets poked.

'Stop it, you dreadful woman!'

With 20 seconds to go in the round, Sue walks back to her cart and hoists herself up into the seat.

'Hey!' I say. 'What are you doing?'

She turns the key, hits the accelerator and starts ripping down the alley. I can't believe that this woman is going to run my grandmother over.

'Nan, get out of the way!' I rush towards her but she has this strange look in her eye.

She holds up a hand to stop me. Sue is about five metres away now and moving in fast. Well, granny-cart fast. Nan's going to get creamed. She grabs her handbag off me and reaches into it with both hands.

'What are you doing?' I take her arm and start pulling, but she wriggles out of my hold, slips on some oven mitts and brings out a container with a lid. It's a casserole dish. She rips off the lid and I see that it's steaming. Sue is only a metre away when Nan lifts the dish and hurls the contents all over the hot-pink cart. Vegetables, meat and a ton of yellow sauce fly through the air and hit Jack's nan.

Sue lets out a bloodcurdler. The cart screeches to a stop, centimetres from my nan. Sue throws herself off the cart and onto the ground. She has sauce all over her head and shoulders. She wipes madly, screaming, 'Get it off me!' Then her dog runs in and starts licking her face and hair. Ponka, my nan's poodle, laps up the food off her shoes.

'Get away from me, you disgusting animals,' she shouts, but the casserole is too delicious and the dogs keep eating. Jack runs in and grabs Sue's dog by the collar but, sure enough, its neck-mouth opens and bites Jack on the hand.

'Yowww!' He pulls his hand back.

Ponka is frightened and runs away.

'*Ding-ding*,' I say. 'End of round two.'

With his unbitten hand, Jack pulls a sweat towel out of his jeans pocket and wipes sauce off Sue's face.

Nan puts the lid on her dish and places it back in her handbag.

'That was awesome!' I say. 'How did you think of that?'

'Always prepared,' she says.

Sue stands and leans against her monster-truck granny cart, her hair and eyebrows thick with sauce. She has bits of carrot and potato on her shoulders and chest. Jack pats at her but she growls at him.

Nan pulls a thermos and two teacups out of her bag and hands the cups to me. She pours the tea and we sip.

I notice the sky is getting lighter. The sun is rising over the bus depot on the other side of the main street.

'I can win this,' Nan says. 'I'm quite enjoying myself now. But we should get it over with before The Fuzz get here.'

'The Fuzz?' I ask.

'The cops, the heat, the boys in blue,' she says.

'I've never heard you talk like this.'

'There are a lot of things you don't know about me, Tom Weekly,' she replies with a wink.

Round Three

Sue is wearing a pair of large, red boxing gloves and matching headgear. She shoves a mouthguard in, shadow-boxing and dancing her way towards Nan.

'I want you!' she says, pointing a glove. Her dog gives a low growl. Ponka hides behind me, shaking.

'Bring it,' Nan says.

Where does she even hear things like, 'bring it'? I wonder.

Sue weaves forward and lands a jab on my nan's chin.

'Oooo,' Nan says, clutching at her jaw.

Then Sue gives her a couple of uppercuts, a right hook and another six or seven quick jabs. She's using my nan's head as a speedbag.

Nan looks over to me, dazed. 'Is that you, Neville?' Neville is my uncle.

'No, it's Tom.'

'Who?'

WHam!

Nan in La-la LAnd.

Sue unleashes another storm of punches.

'Stop it!' I scream. This has gone too far. I don't care if Jack wins.

'S'okay,' my Nan says, groggily stumbling to her right.

'No, it's not.'

Sue gets Nan in a headlock, cutting off her windpipe.

'You rotter!' Nan gasps.

'Say "mercy",' Sue says, 'and it's all over. I won't let you go until I hear it.'

Nan is starting to go blue. Her shirt is pulled up, and the colostomy bag attached to her stomach is showing. Nan's bowels have been on the skids for years, but last year she had to have this plastic bag attached to her belly to collect her poo. I know more than I want to: I had to empty it for her last Sunday before we sat down for roast.

'Say "mercy",' I scream at Nan. 'Say it now!'

But I see something sparkle in my nan's eyes. She reaches into her mouth and pulls out her false teeth. Then she 'bites' Jack's nan on the arm, right on the lizard tattoo. She has the set of teeth chattering on the ends of her fingers.

'Argh,' Jack's nan says. 'Argh, you can't do that! It hurts. Stop it.'

Nan bites Sue on the fingers, then reaches up and bites her on the neck, the cheek, working those teeth like a pair of castanets.

Nan and her big smile

Sue lets go, clutching at her own neck, screeching, 'You can't do that!'

'Who says?' Nan calls, grinning and jamming her teeth back in. 'And, by the way, your blouse looks disgusting. Don't you *own* an iron?'

Sue looks down at herself, then up at Nan.

She looks upset. She looks angry. I guess you don't tell an old woman that her ironing stinks. Sue pulls back her fist, winding up for the haymaker, a punch that will lift Nan off her feet. I want to do something, but it all happens too quickly.

Sue's fist drives forward and hits Nan in the stomach – right in her colostomy bag. When the punch lands there is an almost deafening *POP!* that echoes off the alley walls. The bag has burst, and you don't even want to know what comes out.

Yes, you do.

Poo.

Not a small amount, but a LOT of poo.

And it doesn't just drip out. It *explodes*. The contents of the bag go all over Sue, all over her dog, all over the monster-truck granny cart – and all over Jack. It is the most intense explosion in the history of that disgusting brown substance.

Everything stops. Jack's nan stands there, her fist frozen where it made contact with the colostomy bag. She looks a lot like she did after round two, only this time it's not casserole sauce that's dripping from her eyebrows and chin. The gigantic double-mouthed dog is licking itself madly, like it's just been for a swim in Willy Wonka's chocolate river.

I don't know whether to laugh or cry. Jack and his nan wipe their eyes.

'*Ding-ding.* End of round three,' I say.

Jack looks like he's ready to blow.

Nan dusts her hands together. 'Well, that settles that then. Who wants a cuppa?'

I have the toughest Nan in the world. Think yours can beat her? Bring it.

Our New Game Idea

Jack and I have been working on a new video game idea. It's called *Zombie Dog Spit* and, in it, you have to stay away from a zombie dog. If the dog licks you, you turn into a zombie, too.

Toe

'Tom-Tom, come he-ere!'

That cry sent a shiver down my spine. It was 35 degrees outside but I was covered in goosebumps. I quickly closed the trapdoor, rolled back the rug in the centre of my bedroom floor, stuffed the lollies and comics into my backpack and zipped it up. Then I dropped and rolled under my bed.

'*Tom?*' the voice said, sharper this time. I closed my eyes and sent out a desperate prayer that if I kept quiet she might think I'd left for Jack's place already, that maybe I'd climbed out the window and disappeared into the afternoon.

'I'm getting a little perturbed,' she said a few seconds later. 'I know you're in there. I can smell you.'

My mind raced for answers. But I knew there were none. I slid out from under the bed. I could run but I couldn't hide. She'd find me, and whatever she did to me then would be ten times worse than whatever she had planned for me now. Like the time she texted Sasha and told her that I was in love with her. And the time she put plastic wrap over the toilet seat.

I stood and walked slowly to the door. I pulled it open and peered through the crack. Across the hall I could see her sitting at the dining room table. My sister, Tanya. Evil genius. Four years older than me, hair in a ponytail, grin on her face. There was half a glass of orange juice sitting next to her on the table. She was letting thick, sticky saliva drip down past her chin, then sucking it back up into her mouth, yoyo-style. This was one of her favourite tricks. Sometimes she could let it drip right down to her bellybutton and still vacuum it back up.

'Don't be shy, little friend,' she said, like she was trying to lure a small marsupial out of its home before injuring it in some way. 'C'mon, Tommy. I have something for you.'

My sister - eViL GeNius

beady eyes
(cAn look straigHt through you!)

Maniacal lAugH

sHarp claws

evil...
ah...
ponytail
tHING.

I opened the door a little more, squeezed out, shut it behind me and shuffled across the hall to the dining room. I stopped in the doorway, leaving at least three metres between us. Tanya had a three-metre rule. If I came within three metres of her she'd pull out a chunk of my hair. She'd done it once about a year ago. A small piece of scalp had come away, too.

'Getting ready to go to Little Jacky's place?' she said, hoisting one foot up onto the dining table. Bando, lying on his dog bed in the corner of the room, watched her foot carefully.

'His name's Jack, he's not little, and you know I am,' I said, super-suss.

She looked down at her toe and I could see there was something stuck to it. Something big and black. I looked away, not daring to ask.

'There's just one little thing I need you to do before I let you go,' she said.

'Mum already said I could go. As if I'm doing anything for you.' I was trying to be strong but I was a goldfish to her killer whale.

She laughed. Actually laughed in my face. I tried not to say anything, but it went on and on until I had to ask the question. 'What?'

'I just love it when you try to act tough,' she said. 'If it was anyone else I'd say it was "cute", but it's you so it makes me want to puke.'

'You're adopted,' I said.

'Me? I'm the one who looks like Mum. You just look like some . . . random dude.'

I turned away and headed for my room.

'Eat it or I'll tell Mum about the hole,' she said.

I stopped, my back still turned. I didn't want her to see my face.

'What?'

'Eat the Vegemite off my toe or I'll call Mum and tell her about the hole that you sawed in the middle of your bedroom floor. It's hidden by the rug and you hide lollies in it.'

I turned, looked her dead in the eye.

3 things I'd rather do than eat vegemite off my sister's toe

1. Saw my own arm off.

2. Eat a bowl of cockroaches

3. Suck the pus out of Lisa Crabapple's zits

Almost in a whisper, I said, 'How did you know about the hole?'

'I know everything,' she said. 'Now eat the 'mite or I'm calling.'

Bando stood and jumped up, resting his paws on Tanya's lap, trying to eat the Vegemite off her toe. 'Get down!' she barked at him, shoving him away roughly and brushing fur off her uniform.

I looked at her foot again. The gooey stuff was definitely Vegemite. It was like a small scoop of black ice-cream perched right on top of her big toe.

'As if I'm going to eat something off your toe,' I said.

She picked the phone up off the

dining table. I couldn't believe she was going to do this. Well, actually, I could. This was exactly the kind of thing that she would do.

'I thought you didn't like me going near you,' I said. 'Think about it for a second. I'd actually have to touch you if I ate that Vegemite.'

She looked up from the phone and blinked. Just once. It wasn't much but I knew I'd hit a nerve. She sat there for a minute, chewing it over, trying to keep a straight face, nervously dripping juice yoyos down her chin and sucking them back up.

'As you know,' she said, 'I don't even like being in the same room as you. But, just this once, I'm prepared to make an exception. So lap it up.'

I looked at her. I looked at the toe.

'Fine,' I said. 'I don't care. Call Mum.' I turned and headed for my room again. I heard the first beep as my hand hit the door handle. Then there was a slow series of beeps as she dialled. Oh well. I didn't mind. So what? Mum'd find out about my trapdoor. Big deal.

She'd pressed five numbers. Three more and she'd have a connection.

Beep.

Six numbers. I mean, who cares that Mum had been trying to sell the place for a year? The new owner would just have to put a new floor in. Simple.

Beep.

Or maybe they could build a cellar underneath the house?

Beep.

I turned to her. She was looking at me, phone to ear.

'Hello, can I please speak to Catherine Weekly? . . . Okay, thanks.'

She's bluffing, I thought.

'You're totally bluffing,' I said.

'Hi, Mum,' she said, waiting, listening.

'Yeah, we're good.'

She looked and sounded suspiciously like she was really talking to Mum.

'There's a little problem with Tom, though.'

Now I could actually *hear* my mother's voice on the other end of the phone.

'He's done something,' she said. 'I've been meaning to tell you for a while.'

I walked across the hall towards her, shaking my head.

'Well,' she said, smiling. 'He's been in his room ...'

I put my hands together, begging her not to say anything. I pointed to the toe and nodded my head, licking my lips, rubbing my belly.

'And he's cleaned it all up,' she said. 'It looks *really* good.'

I heard Mum say something.

'Yeah, I was proud, too. Anyway, just wanted to let you know ... Love you ... Bye ...'

She hung up. She wiggled her toes. She pointed to an empty seat. I sat. I looked at the toe in close-up. Her grinning face was a blur in the background. She took a slow sip of orange juice and then did the longest saliva stretchy I'd ever seen. On the way back up it hung right out to the side, almost around to her ear, before – 'SSSSSLP!' – she hoovered it back into her gob. It was almost a 'Round the World'. If there was a Gross Olympics then she just won gold. I was waiting for the national anthem.

But the toe twitched and I looked at it again. I could mainly see the underside. There were little bits of dry skin flaking off. I looked around to the edge of the toenail and I could see scratchy scraps of black nail polish. There was definitely some kind of carbuncle on the side, too. I didn't exactly know what a carbuncle was, but I had a sick feeling that this was one.

I shook my head. 'I can't,' I said. I stood up.

She grabbed the phone, lightning quick, like she was drawing it from a holster.

Beep. Beep. Beep.

I sat back down on the chair. She ended the call. I looked at the toe again. She grinned. I sniffed. The foot had a sweaty, been-at-school-in-a-shoe-all-day stink to it. I eyed off the Vegemite – a golf ball of concentrated yeast extract sitting on top of the toe. Even making me eat that much Vege off a spoon would have been sick and wrong. To serve it on a festy toe took a mind so evil that she could have been in a Batman comic. The Joker, Mr Freeze and My Sister.

'Tombles! Eat!' she growled. 'Three seconds. Three . . .'

I swallowed hard.

'Two.'

I licked my lips, tensed my fists, clenched my jaw.

'One.'

I closed my eyes, opened my mouth, tried to tell myself it was just Vegemite ice-cream. I took a deep breath and ...

I couldn't do it. It was too disgusting.

WHACK! Tanya hit me on the back of the head, my teeth closed around the toe and I bit down hard.

I didn't mean to, but I heard tendon and bone snap, like a dog chomping on a chicken wing. She screamed next-suburb loud and stood up, her foot still in my mouth.

Then the final crunch and the toe came away. I screamed. I had my sister's toe in my mouth. And it wasn't connected to her foot. This was not part of my plan for the afternoon. All I wanted was to go to Jack's, and now I was chewing on a big, festy toe that tasted like school. I could only think of one thing to do . . . I took the toe out of my mouth and offered it to her.

She screamed even louder. She didn't have
to get so upset. I was just trying to be nice.
I was the one who should have been angry.
She'd threatened to reveal my secret, messed
up my whole afternoon, hit me on the back
of the head.

You really ought to cut your nails. I could've got a nasty cut on my tongue.

I mean, I couldn't exactly
head off to Jack's. I'd have to call the doctor,
call Mum, wait around. This could take hours.

I wondered if I should put the toe on ice.

Or if I should hide it in my trapdoor. No,
that'd be weird.

Maybe I should offer to sew it back on.

Although I've never officially sewn anything before.

Then, out of nowhere, Bando jumped off his bed, lightning-quick, grabbed the toe in his jaws, and bolted off through the kitchen and out the back door.

My mouth fell open.

Tanya fell to the ground.

'Go!' she shouted.

I chased Bando into the yard. By the time I caught sight of him he was three-quarters of the way to freedom through the hole at the back near the shed. I ran and dived, just grabbing his tail. I thought I had him but then that rod of wiry fur slipped through my fingers as he wriggled his way out into the world, and then he was gone.

What was I supposed to do? And what was I going to say to Mum? Sorry, but I accidentally bit Tanya's toe off and then the dog ate it?

There was no way I'd be going to Jack's now. My life was officially over, and it was all Tanya's fault.

Big sisters can be so thoughtless sometimes.

If You *Had* to Eat Something Off Your Sister's Crusty Toe (Like It Was Life or Death), What Would You Eat? I Asked My Class. This Is What They Said:

* Marshmallow
* Lettuce
* A toenail
* A cookie
* A praying mantis

* Cream cheese
* Sock juice
* Nutella
* A kebab
* Snot

Scab

Three days ago, 2.51 pm, our whole class
was sitting on the floor at the front of the
classroom listening to a story. I was staring at
a scab, the biggest I'd ever seen. It was wafer
thin and golden brown, like a perfectly baked
Anzac biscuit. Delicious almost. It was lifted
slightly at the edges. I could rip it off in one
quick movement. I knew I could. It wouldn't
even bleed. It would look incredible in my
scab collection. I just wished it was on my
knee instead of Jack's.

'Sir, could we please see the pictures?' Jack
asked.

Mr Skroop, the teacher filling in for Miss Norrish for a few weeks, was reading us a book. It was a fantasy novel with a picture every few pages. I'm about the only kid in my year who doesn't like fantasy books. The scab was much more interesting.

Skroop glared over his glasses at Jack, pursing

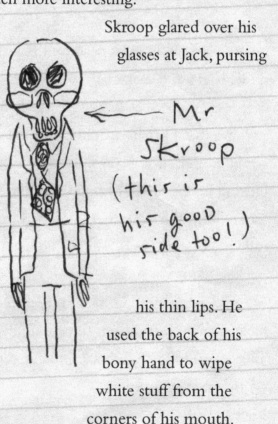

Mr Skroop (this is his good side too!)

his thin lips. He used the back of his bony hand to wipe white stuff from the corners of his mouth.

Jack gulped. He should have known by now not to mess with Skroop. Nobody in the room breathed for a few seconds.

Skroop continued reading. He still didn't show us the pictures, and he read so fast that you could hardly catch the words. Unlike other teachers, Mr Skroop seemed to not like books. Or kids. He was dead on the inside. Just spider shells and snake tails.

I looked down at Jack's scab again. It was so loose that I bet he would hardly even feel it coming off. Jack was staring at the ceiling and picking his ear. I had to find exactly the right moment. In the story there was a creature called The Squandrel creeping along a forest track, looking for prey.

'Searching, hunting,' said Skroop in a lifeless voice. 'It had been three long days since The Squandrel had eaten.' I listened, carefully waiting for my moment.

'Boo!'

Something jumped out from behind a tree in the story. The kids gasped. I ripped the scab. Jack screamed, loud. Then he punched me in the arm. Skroop stopped reading and looked at Jack. I pocketed the scab.

'WHAT was that?' he asked.

I knew Jack would cover for me. There was no way he'd dob me in to Skroop.

'Tom ripped the scab off my knee!' he squealed, pointing at me. I looked to my right, trying to make out like Jack was pointing to some other Tom.

'Tom Weekly. OUT!' Skroop said.

'But I –'

'Oouuuuuuuut!'

I stood and accidentally kicked Jack really hard in the ankle as I walked past.

'Stand with your nose to the wall in the corridor and then see me after the lesson. Book time is SPECIAL!' he screamed. 'I won't have it ruined.'

I spent 20 minutes sniffing the wall in the hall before the bell rang for the end of school. The class walked past me, looking miserable. Jack picked up his bag and said, 'Gimme my scab.'

'No way. That baby's going in my book,' I said. 'I can't believe you dobbed me in.'

Skroop appeared in the doorway. He made a *come here* motion with one knotted, dinosaur finger and then headed back inside.

I gulped and followed. He sat down at his desk, poured a cup of tea from a thermos and took an unopened packet of biscuits from his bag. Iced VoVos. He placed them on his desk.

'Looking at me please, Mr Weekly, not at my biscuits,' he said. 'Did I overhear in the hallway that you have a scab collection?'

I looked at the floor and nodded.

'I, too, had a scab collection when I was a boy,' he said.

I looked up. 'That's good,' I said, thinking how creepy it was.

'Give me the scab.' He held out one bony hand.

I looked at him for a moment. Did he really want it? I had to think quickly. 'I gave it back to Jack.'

He watched me darkly, like he was about to make me empty my pockets but, after what seemed like forever, he said, 'You will spend every lunchtime with me in the classroom until you have read this entire novel, do you understand?' He held up a copy of *The Squandrel*. I hung my head. My worst nightmare.

'Yes,' I mumbled.

'Yes, what?'

'Yes, Mr Skroop.'

'And you will give me a daily report at the end of each detention.'

'Yes, sir,' I said.

'Now go and catch your bus, Weekly. I shall see you tomorrow.'

I turned and headed for the door, running my finger over the rough surface of the scab in my pocket. I already knew that I wasn't going to show up for detention. I just needed a plan.

my favourite scab dream...

what A beAutY!

'Where does it hurt?' Mum asked, sitting on the edge of my bed the next morning.

'Just sort of there,' I said, rubbing the right side of my stomach, just above my hip.

She poked it with her fingers and I said, 'Ow.' She looked at me and I tried to give her my best pain-face. She poked it again. I said, 'Ow.'

Poke.

'Ow.'

Poke.

'Ow.'

She looked suspicious. 'Well, we'll have to take you to the doctor. Even though it'll make me late for work.'

She was testing. She knew I didn't like going to the doctor, but I was more scared of Skroop.

'Okay,' I said in a husky voice.

She growled and stood, turning to me at my bedroom door. She knew there was something weird about the way I was acting.

'Alright, I'll call now,' but she stayed there, giving me one last chance to say, 'No, I'll be okay.' But I thought about The Squandrel and

I thought about Skroop. In my mind, Skroop was becoming The Squandrel.

'Alrighty then,' I said.

She looked annoyed and left the room.

I jumped out of bed and pulled on my school shorts from yesterday. The scab was still in my pocket. I figured I'd take it with me, for good luck.

'Jump up on the bed for me, Tom,' Dr Pellow said. He was an old guy with a sunburnt face and one gold tooth, right at the front. He'd been our family doctor for, like, 250 years.

I sat up on the hard bed with the red leather cover. I strained as though it hurt to climb up. Mum rolled her eyes and looked at her watch.

'Hands to the side please,' the doc said. 'Cough for me.'

I coughed.

'How does that feel?'

'Bit sore,' I said, resting a hand on my stomach.

He pressed where I'd pointed. 'And how is that?'

I pulled a face and sucked in a sharp breath, careful not to overdo it. Mum was watching my every move.

'And that?' he said, looking over his glasses at me.

'Ow,' I said.

We went on like this for a while. I don't like to boast but my performance was pretty good. I'd get a day off for sure. Maybe two. Hopefully, by then, old Skroopers might have forgotten the detention.

'Okay, you can jump down for me now,' Dr Pellow said.

I carefully got off the bed.

The doctor went over to his desk and scratched something on his pad. Awesome.

Prescription. That meant medicine, which probably meant a day off while it was doing its thing. I couldn't believe how easy this had been – like taking candy from a baby. I could even fool a doctor into thinking I was sick. Maybe I needed to consider acting as a career.

'What do you think it is?' my mum asked.

I put my hand in my pocket and my finger touched the scab, my treasure. It was still in one big, beautiful piece. I would stick it in my book as soon as I got home.

'I think,' said Dr Pellow, 'that we have a possibly severe case of appendicitis.'

'Right,' Mum said. She looked worried for the first time. 'And what should we do?'

'I think,' he said, 'that we had better get this boy down to the hospital and take his appendix out, quick sticks.' He finished writing on the pad, took off his glasses, tore off the piece of paper and handed it to Mum.

'Are you sure?' I said.

'I've been practising for 45 years. I've diagnosed thousands of appendicitis cases and you're showing classic symptoms. The abdominal wall is sensitive to palpation. There's rebound tenderness. Pain in the right iliac fossa. I suggest we take it out.'

He walked to the door. We followed.

'So that means an operation?' I asked.

I'm Afraid we're going to have to open your guts up and cut a WHole bunch of stuff out of You. 'Pain and blood' Are tHe words that come to mind. OH, and 'icky' too. Not. MucH. fuN. No.

'Well, we won't get it out by magic. Don't worry – I'm sure there'll be lots of ice-cream afterwards. What's your favourite flavour?'

I didn't want ice-cream from this maniac. I wanted my body parts.

'Maybe we can just see what happens,' I said. 'It's sort of feeling a bit better already. Look.' I poked myself in the belly and grinned.

Dr P. smiled, too. 'Don't worry. You'll be asleep. It'll be a little uncomfortable for a couple of days but you'll be back on the football pitch before you know it. I'll see you in about ten days to remove your stitches.'

'But –' I said.

'Bye-bye now.' He closed the door on us. I looked at Mum. She was worried.

'C'mon, mate. We'd better get you to the hospital.' She put an arm around me. 'I thought you were pretending.'

'I was!' I said as we walked through the waiting room. 'I'm fine.'

'I just have to ring work. Quiet for a minute.'

She paid the receptionist while she made the call.

My head was swirling. What had I done? How was I going to get out of this? All I wanted was a day off school. Now some dude was going to hack me up and rip my guts out. All because of Skroop.

In the car I explained to Mum what a mistake this was, that I was okay now. When we arrived at the hospital, walking across the car park, I beat my stomach with my fists.

'See, it doesn't hurt at all!'

'It's okay, mate. It'll be over quickly. Like Dr Pellow said, you won't feel a thing.'

We walked in through the sliding front doors of the reception area. There were people lined up in rows of orange seats. People who actually looked sick. They had white faces and bags under their eyes. Some of them were

random thoughts About my operation

1. Will I be nude?
   1a. If 'Yes', then will I be Awake?
2. What if they open me up and a small animal jumps in without anyone noticing?! (like a hamster or a small dog.)
3. Will I get stitches or a zipper?
4. Can mum video* the operation for 'NEWS' at school? (that would be pretty cool!)
5. Will my screAming distrAct the Doctor?

* remember to recharge video camerA!
(Unless Answer to question 1 is yes.)

114

bleeding. There were kids screaming and old people drooling. This wasn't a place to get better. I'd probably catch something rare and incurable here.

Mum spoke to the receptionist and we waited for ages for a nurse to arrive. I was a fox in a hole, a rat in a trap. I needed to gnaw my way out. I was usually a genius in these situations. Maybe I could cry? Brilliant. I threw myself on the ground and started bawling.

'Oh, get up! Stop pretending and don't be such a baby,' Mum snapped.

I peeled myself off the floor, scanning my mind for the best excuse I'd ever come up with. My life was on the line.

Boom.

'I have to go to school,' I said. 'I've got this special lunchtime reading club with Mr Skroop. It's the first day and I'd better not miss it. It's just me and him in the club so far.'

'I thought you didn't like him.'

'No, he's changed. He's good. He's great! And I have to go because –'

'It's okay. I'll call the school,' she said.

'No, but –'

A nurse arrived with a wheelchair.

'Hello, I'm Merrill. You must be Tom. If you can hop up in the chair for me we'll have the doctor take a look at you.' She was speaking to me like I was a five-year-old. I didn't need a wheelchair. I wanted to be at school, sitting at my desk reading *The Squandrel*. I wanted to spend some quality time with good old Mr Skroop, my favourite teacher. Suddenly I loved fantasy books. I wanted to read the entire Lord of the Rings trilogy in Elvish language. For fun. I tried to explain this to my mother as they wheeled me down a long corridor. We went through about 27 sets of double doors into an area that was like a parking bay. They got me to change into a hospital gown and jump up on a bed. Over the next five minutes, kids were wheeled in and out. Some of them looked like they had already been under the knife. I had to get out of there. These lunatics were going to slice 'n' dice me. I sat up, ready to run, but the nurse grabbed my arm and jabbed a needle into it.

'Just something to help you relax,' she said.

I was going to tell her where to stick her needle next but things sort of went fuzzy. Then she put another needle in my arm and tied it to a board with a bandage. A clear rubber tube ran from my arm up to a plastic bag with clear liquid in it. Then I was wheeled down another long corridor, around corners. More sets of doors. They were trying to confuse me so I couldn't escape. I tried to count the fluoro lights that flickered by above me so I'd know how to get back, but I lost count.

'Stop,' I said, but my voice sounded far

away. I wanted to get up and explain to the
nurse that I was just trying to get out of
detention with Skroop. I'd made the whole
thing up. Surely she could remember doing
stuff like that when she was a kid. But I
couldn't move or speak.

The bed came to rest. There was a really
bright, round light above me. I lay there for a
few minutes. My mum wasn't there anymore,
but a doctor wearing a mask was looking
down at me. 'How are we today, Tom?'

'Not good,' I said, but it was slurred and
sounded more like, 'Nod goo.'

'Just count backwards from ten for me,
thanks Tom.'

'Nine,' I said. 'Six . . . Three . . .' Everything
went warm and dark.

The end
of an era

So long
world!

Goodbye my
old friend.

I woke up here. In a hospital ward. Pain yelped from my belly, just above the hip. I knew right away that they'd taken one of my favourite body parts. I'd never really thought about my appendix before, but now that it was gone I really missed it.

gone I really missed it.

I turned over onto my left side.

I screamed.

Not because of the pain but because sitting there, staring at me, was Skroop. Maybe I was still asleep, having a nightmare. Skroop didn't belong at the hospital. He should have been at the graveyard scaring zombies or back in the classroom terrorising kids. He held up a copy of *The Squandrel* and I screamed again.

My mum appeared behind him at the door of the ward. She smiled. I didn't smile back.

'Hello, darling,' she said. 'What are you screaming for? It's Mr Skroop. I told him how upset you were at the thought of missing Lunchtime Book Club and he offered to come down after school to see you.'

I looked directly into Skroop's black, soulless eyes. He smiled a sickly, thin-lipped smile. He knew there was no book club. With one knuckly, knotted hand, he passed me *The Squandrel*.

'Here,' he said. 'I'll drop by each afternoon to read you a passage.'

'No, it's okay,' I whispered. 'I don't want to put you to any trouble.'

'No, it's no trouble. It's on my way home

from school. And your idea of a lunchtime book club is excellent. Maybe a fantasy book club, hey? You can be my first member.' In my head I heard his laughter, *Mwahahahahahaha*.

He stood and smiled at me with those thin, porridge lips. 'For now, you rest up.'

'Say thank you,' Mum said.

'Ugoo,' I grunted.

Skroop turned for the door. Mum followed, thanking him so much for coming. I lay there, trying to understand what had just happened. My life was a mess.

I looked over and saw a vase of yellow flowers on the bedside table. My school shorts were neatly folded right next to it. They reminded me of something. Jack's scab. If there was one good thing to come from all this it was that I would be adding the biggest, most beautiful scab I'd ever seen to my collection. I half-smiled and reached up, sending a jagged knife of pain into my stomach. I groaned and grabbed the shorts. I rested them on my chest and reached into the pocket, waiting to feel that thin, crispy goodness. Wrong pocket. I tried the other one. I even tried the back pockets but found nothing.

'Bye-bye,' Mum said to Skroop as she headed across the room towards my bed. But Skroop didn't leave. He stayed there in the doorway behind Mum, staring at me. He took something out of his pocket. It was wafer thin and golden brown, like a perfectly baked Anzac biscuit.

I watched carefully as Skroop did something unspeakable. He put the thing in his mouth and chewed it up. I had been given detention and lost a body part for that scab and now it was gone, eaten by my teacher. When he finished he wiped the corners of his mouth with a gnarled pinkie finger.

'Cheerio then,' Skroop said. 'See you tomorrow.' And he disappeared down the hall.

Ralph

I've been working on my own comic. This is my main character, Ralph. What do you think? Have you ever made one?

what Are YOU looking at?!

RalPH, The baDDest BeAr oN tHe plAnet!

Swoop

I'm walking down my street. I have an ice-cream container on my head. The container has eyes painted on the back of it and sticks poking out at weird angles. I can see kids at the bus stop through the rough-cut eyeholes. They're laughing at me. Even Sasha, the cutest girl in Australia, who is supposed to be my girlfriend as of yesterday, is laughing. But I don't care. I've had enough. I've been swooped too many times.

'The ice-cream man is coming!' someone calls. 'Where's your truck, ice-cream man?'

'I'll have a choc top,' someone else shouts,

'with hundreds and thousands.'

They're real comedians, the kids on my street.

Some dude screams, 'Watch out! Magpie!' and points into the sky. But I'm so not falling for that old trick.

WHAM! The bird hits me, knocking the container off my head. Kids howl with laughter. I hit the ground and the maggie comes back for a second swoop. It's deadly accurate, pecking me right in the middle of the forehead. Blood gushes from my head and dribbles down my face onto the grass. No one is laughing now. They are standing, mouths open, watching me. Except Sasha. She turns the other way, embarrassed. It hurts.

Ice - Cream Man

I am a magnet for magpies. I've been attacked three times in the past week, and it isn't even spring yet. I've been swooped hundreds of times in my life and pecked about eight. I have three scars on my forehead, four on my scalp and one on my nose. I swear it's the same magpie in the same spot every

Scars of a man at WAR

MondAy (afternoon)

THursday

MonDay (morning)

FridAy (this one hurt!)

TUEsday

Wednesda

today

year – top of the telegraph pole right in front
of my house.

Now Sasha thinks I'm a total lame-o, and
there aren't that many other girls lining up to
go out with me. None, actually. I swear this is
the last time I'm going to let this happen.

'I think we should move,' I say to Mum,
looking up from my homework that night.

'So do I, but no one will buy the house,'
she says, dipping her finger into the spaghetti
sauce to see if it's ready. 'I thought you loved
this house. Why do you want to move?'

'No reason,' I say.

She looks at me. 'It's the magpie, isn't it?'

'No,' I say, running my thumb over the
white surgical patch on my forehead.

'They're not vicious animals. They're just
protecting their babies. That's what they're
programmed to do.'

'Did you get swooped again?' my sister asks, coming into the kitchen. She dumps her netball stuff on the ground and kisses Mum. 'Sucked in. If I was a magpie I'd swoop you, too.'

'Tanya!' Mum snaps.

'Why's he such a loser? Who gets swooped by the same magpie every single day? Why doesn't he just walk a different way?'

'It's right in front of the house,' Mum says.

'Well, I don't get swooped.'

'It probably heads south for the winter when it sees your face,' I say.

'I don't like you,' Tanya says. 'The bird doesn't like you. When are you going to get the message?'

'Will you two please −'

'What do you mean "you two"?' I say to Mum. 'I didn't −'

'You always have to keep it going, Tom. Go to your room and come back when you're −'

'But –'

'Room!' Mum demands.

I throw a pen at Tanya. It misses. I leave.

In my bedroom I peel back the blind just a crack to see if the maggie is there. It's right on dusk but I can see it out there on top of the pole, shoulders hunched against the darkness. At that moment the bird turns and looks at me. It's like it senses my every move. Its beady red eyes glow, glaring at me over that nasty, bloodthirsty beak.

'You're trying to ruin my life,' I say quietly. I have a giant gash on my forehead. I've been ridiculed by my sister and sent to my room. Sasha told me at school that she won't speak to me until I stop humiliating her. It's all because of that bird. At this time of year it doesn't even have babies to protect. It's the middle of winter. This is no ordinary magpie doing natural magpie stuff. This is personal.

BOY versus

WILD!

SCORECARD

Wild: 27
Boy: 0

It's Me versus It. Boy versus Wild.

In that moment I decide to go deep
undercover. Between leaving the house and
arriving at the bus stop tomorrow morning,
no bird, no living thing, will know where I
am. Look up 'invisible' in the dictionary and
there'll be a picture of me. (Although I'll
be invisible so I guess the picture will be of
whatever is behind me.) I'm ready to heal my
scars, win back my pride and let Sasha know
that I'm made of awesome.

'Seeya,' I call to Mum as I head out the back
door.

'Where are you going?'

'School.'

'Why out the back? And what are you
wearing? Where's your uniform?'

I let the door slam.

'Whatever you're up to,' she calls, 'you'd

better move it! Four minutes till the bus.'

I scooch down low and dart across the yard to the base of our tall timber fence. Bando dances around my feet, trying to get me to throw a drool-soaked plastic hamburger for him. 'Shoo!' I say, and I hide in the low hedge. I'm dressed all in green – green trackies, an old green long-sleever and a green cap with mould on it that I found in the laundry. My uniform is underneath.

I peer through the hedge, along the side of our house, to see the enemy on top of his pole out front. Back turned. Perfect. Time for me to disappear. I reach for the top of the fence and pull myself up with a grunt. I slip over and down the other side into our neighbour Lisa's garden. I fall to my belly and sniper crawl through the long grass till I'm out of enemy sight. I'm doing pretty well until halfway across the yard when Frisbee, Lisa's dog, starts barking.

'Sssshhhh, ssssshhhhh,' I whisper. 'Quiet! It's just me, Fris.'

But The Fris keeps yapping as she speeds towards me from her kennel near the back door. She is small and white, a lap dog, but she looks kind of vicious right now, baring her tiny, razor-sharp teeth. She doesn't like me much and I can't take any more of this barking. I make a dash for the next yard. Just as I reach the fence, she nips me on the ankle. I throw myself over into a garden bed filled with pink and white rose bushes. I peel my sock down and check my ankle. It has little teeth marks on it and specks of blood.

Something moves at the corner of my vision. It's the magpie swooping into the mango tree in our backyard. It leans forward on its toes, eyes alert, wings slightly raised, ready to strike.

'Thanks,' I whisper to Frisbee, who is still yapping at me through the fence.

Only two more yards after this and I'll be at Sasha's. Then I'll just bolt down the side of her house to the bus stop.

'What are you doing in my garden, boy?' says a voice.

Nuts. It's the old man with the wild white hair and the crazy eyes, the one who washes his car every day but never drives it. He's calling to me from his kitchen window.

My eyes flick between him and the bird.

'Get out of my roses,' he says. 'You'll damage them.' He disappears from the window as though he's coming outside. I run across his yard, top speed, leapfrogging the birdbath. I wait for the dreaded flap of wings right behind my ears. But it doesn't come.

I grab the top of two fence posts and launch myself over. I lay low, peering through the fence as the old man comes out into his yard. 'Boy!' he says.

The bird has disappeared from the mango

tree. A bit of Weet-Bix rises up into my throat. I have about a minute to get to the bus stop. I still have this yard and Sasha's to go and the bird is missing in action.

It's quiet. Too quiet. I don't like it. I spin around and see a blur of black and white streaking through the air. I search for its dark red eyes among that smudge of feathers. I get a lock on them and then the enemy does something totally unexpected – it freaks. Just for a second there is panic in its eyes. The bird swoops up into a tall gum tree. The tree hangs over a rusty, dark green shed on the other side of the yard, near Sasha's fence.

My eyes are glued to the bird. I'm going to watch it all the way to the bus stop. My eyeballs are its kryptonite. I pretty much have to go underneath the tree to get over Sasha's fence, but that's okay. I take steady steps forward, nice and easy, eye to eye. Seconds later I bang into the garden shed. I lose concentration for a moment and take my eyes off the bird.

Whoo, whoo, whoo. Snap, snap, snap. I feel the flap of wings and snap of beak behind me. My cat-like reflexes kick in and I reach a hand up to the back of my head, trying to grab a wing or a foot. I feel feathers on my fingertips, then a scratch of claw across my hand. I turn, looking into the sky – feathers, branches and sunlight. Panicking, I quickly slide the shed door across, slip inside and close myself in.

I'm panting hard, head thumping. The shed is dark. I can see the outline of machinery and boxes. I can smell petrol. I turn, bumping rakes and brooms that clatter to the ground. For a moment everything is quiet.

I listen.

The bus turns the corner onto Kingsley from Grand Street. There's no way I'm going to make it to the stop unless I bolt right now. Bird above me, hiding in a dark, creepy shed, still a yard to go, bus coming. This is it. If I miss this bus I won't be sitting next to Sasha on the way to school. Mum will go mental because I'll be late and she'll have to drive me and, worst of all, I will know that I've been beaten again. By a bird.

I open the door just a crack and peer up into the tree. The maggie is sitting on the lowest branch, giving me demonic red eyes of death.

'You feathered FREAK!' I call to it. But it doesn't care. It starts doing that yodelling thing that magpies do. Within seconds, four magpies swoop and land in the tree. My heart sinks. The bird keeps yodelling and another three magpies join him. I've only just finished counting the eight that are there when five or six more land on nearby branches. This can't be happening. There is an army of birds, crouched, ready to eat me alive. I read somewhere that magpies can gang up like this

when they're trying to catch a falcon or an
owl. I'm so gone.

The call of the magpie...

MwAh
hahaha
haha
haha ha
haha
haha

I do a quick bird-count. Thirteen. Thirteen
bloodthirsty 'pies in a tree. Sounds like a
nursery rhyme. I make a mental note to write
the song if I get out of this alive.

These are my options:

1) Stay in the shed all day.

2) Scream out, 'Mama,' and suck my thumb.

3) Invent a magpie catcher out of stuff I find
   in the shed.

4) Go out and tell a joke: 'What goes black, white, black, white, black, white, red? A magpie burying it's beak in my skull.'

5) Dress up as a magpie and try to fool them that I'm their leader.

6) Dig a tunnel from here to the bus stop.

7) Set the shed on fire and wait to be rescued by the fire department.

But none of these things will get me on that bus next to Sasha. I listen carefully. Brakes squeak as the bus pulls in to the stop.

This is it. I have to run. This is the moment I stop being a boy and become a man. I'm ten times bigger than these dudes. All they have are wings and a beak. (Twenty-six wings and thirteen beaks to be exact.) But I'm human. I'm king of the jungle, and if I want to kick some magpie butt and catch a bus I'll do it.

I feel around on the floor of the shed. I

pick up a plastic rake and carefully peel the door open. It squeals on rusty railings. I take a deep breath and pray. I hold the rake above my head and run, screaming as loud as I can. It's enough to make a magpie's ears bleed. I don't look up. I make a beeline for Sasha's place. The sprinklers are on in her yard but I don't care. I leap the fence.

The first bird swoops. I swing the rake and it soars away. There's another one right behind it, a baby bird in training, who snaps its beak like a woodpecker as I land in Sasha's yard.

I bolt towards the path at the side of her house. The sprinklers soak me as a third bird swoops. Its wing feathers scrape the side of my head. I feel something warm on my shoulder and realise it has pooed on me. I'm running, screaming, waving a rake, wiping poop. I look behind. Five 'pies are bearing down on me. One bumps the side of my head like a shark about to go in for the kill. Another lands on

my backpack.
I spin and
flick it off.
It flies
away.
I have
birds all
over me. I am
Birdman.

I run up the
concrete path. There
are no sprinklers here. I
reach for the top of
the chest-high gate at
the side of the house
and launch myself over. I glance backwards as I
land. There are seven magpies ripping towards
me, single-file, like planes ready to land at a
busy airport. I roll onto my back and bat them
away with the rake. If there were such a thing
as magpie cricket I'd be the Australian captain.

birdMan

I scramble to my feet and run. I reach Sasha's front yard just as the last kid gets on the bus. The sprinklers are on here, too, so I get soaked a second time as I whirl and spin, scanning the sky for magpies. But they've disappeared. I see one sweep high into a tree in the next yard, but that's it.

The bus starts to pull away.

'Wa-a-a-a-a-a-i-t!' I scream, running towards the front gate. I slip on wet grass and land in a puddle, soaking my bottom. I drag myself up and run out onto the footpath.

The bus stops.

Every kid is looking out the window at me. Some are stunned. Others point and laugh, saying things that I can't hear through the glass. I see Sasha, three seats from the front – white jumper, hair in a ponytail, eyes like blue sky. I stand there, out of breath, soaking wet, in my green camouflage gear, with a dog-bitten leg, a claw-scratched hand, a bird-pooed shoulder, a muddy bottom, still wearing a surgical patch on my forehead and clutching a rake.

But I haven't been pecked. I'm not bleeding. Thirteen magpies could not take me down. I've survived. I smile, hoping that Sasha might see the funny side of this. She looks right at me and writes 'I ♥ U' on the bus window in lipstick. I'm so happy I want to scream. She loves me, even if I am a little weird.

The bus door hisses open.

My mind flashes with images of the three kids Sasha and I will have and the labradoodle and the house overlooking the ocean with secret passages and revolving bookcases. Sasha starts writing more words on the window. First she writes: 'Not.' Then she writes: 'Loser.' Her smile is suddenly gone.

'You're not gettin' on my bus like that,' the driver shouts. I walk towards him, trying to explain, but the door closes on me. The bus starts to pull away. Sasha's not watching me anymore, but I can still see those words scrawled on the window. A kid screams, 'Bye-bye freaky bird guy,' as the bus turns the corner and Sasha disappears from my life.

A magpie flutters down from a tree. It doesn't swoop. It just lands on the ground in front of me. It's my magpie. This is the first time I've ever had a really good look at him. He has a black head, a white patch on his neck and long, strong legs. His beak seems to take up almost the entire front of his small head but he doesn't look as nasty as he usually does. And, for some reason, he isn't attacking me. Maybe things have changed between us. Maybe he respects what I've done. It would be hard not to respect a dude who had survived a thirteen-magpie assault.

I look up to make sure that the other birds aren't about to blitz me but they're nowhere to be seen. I bend down and say, 'Hey, fella.' I make that smooching sound that people make to attract possums and stuff. I move in a little closer, just slowly so I don't scare him. I get to within about a metre and I say, 'Friends?'

He watches me curiously and tilts his head to one side. He looks kind of nice, like he's smiling almost. I reach out and he looks for a moment, then takes a step towards me. It feels like we're finally going to connect and put this whole thing to rest. Then WHAM! He flaps his wings hard, lands on my chest and drives his beak into my cheek, real deep. I scream. He flits off into the sky. I drop to my knees, clutching my face, blood dripping through my fingers. The bird yodels his victory song from somewhere in a nearby tree.

I lie down on the grass, staring at the sky. It is clear and blue and, in that moment, I am hit by an idea, a plan for tomorrow morning. It involves a cardboard cut-out of me, a length of rope and a pulley. I can see it so clearly in my mind and, even with the pain screaming through my cheek, a smile slowly spreads across my face.

I swear this is the last time I'm going to let this happen. I'm ready to heal my scars, win back my pride and let Sasha know that I'm made of awesome.

Interesting things I Have learned About Magpies

1. They are <u>very</u> protective of tHeir babies. *

2. THeir beaks could puncture a tractor tyre.

3. They enjoy drawing. Drawing blood.

4. They like curly haired guys wHo answer to the Name of 'Tom'

5. THEY are <u>NOT</u> your friend!

* Even if they don't have Any.

Tooth Job

I needed cash, fast. After six long Sasha-less months she had finally agreed to go see a movie with me on Boxing Day. So, on Christmas Eve, I started my new job – delivering teeth.

'Maybe I don't know enough about teeth?' I said to Mum in the bathroom that morning.

'Well, you have some, don't you? And he's not offering you a job as a dentist,' she said, scrubbing her tongue with the rough rubber back of her toothbrush. She'd just started dating a 'dental prosthetist' – a false-teeth guy. She'd been brushing her teeth six times a day ever since. 'Just, whatever you do, try not to mess this up, Tom. Bryce is a nice man and I need you to do a good job. I think he could be "the one".'

3.30 pm. I stood in front of a wonky wooden house with a sign that read: 'Fensham, Smith and Barrett. Denture Clinic.' Mum was dating Smith. Bryce Smith. A smarmy character with rotten, yellow teeth, strangely enough. I thought about running, but then I thought about

My cousin Rachel...

could eat an apple through a tennis racquet.

Sasha. I thought about sitting next to her in the movies. I'd never been to the movies with a girl before. I said a prayer and shoved open the waiting-room door.

'Hello, do you have an appointment?' asked the receptionist, a youngish woman with a large mole, like a blueberry, at the base of her nose.

'No, I'm ah . . .'

'Thomas!' boomed a voice from down the hall.

I turned and there was Bryce, grinning and flashing those yellow, zigzag babies at me. He grabbed my hand and shook it firmly.

'I'll be taking care of you this afternoon!' He was so excited. I felt like I'd won something. I guess he wanted to impress me so I'd tell Mum what an awesome guy he was.

'Come on' he said, bouncing off down the hall. 'Let's do this.'

He led me into a back room where there

were rows and rows of teeth, all lined up in plastic containers. They looked pretty creepy without mouths.

'Now,' said Smith, 'you need to deliver the dentures on this rack before 5.30. Being Christmas, it's of utmost importance that we distribute them this afternoon or our patients will be toothless under the tinsel and quite cranky about it.'

'How will I carry them?' I asked. 'There are, like, 30 sets of teeth.'

'Ah, the delivery vehicle.' He pointed to an ancient pink bike in the corner. It was pink! Behind it was a two-wheeled trailer, a metre long and about as high as the bike seat. Smith flicked open little doors on either side of the trailer, revealing four racks.

'Slot the containers into the racks, and remember to close the doors carefully. We don't want teeth flying out, do we?' he said, wiggling his wild black-and-silver eyebrows.

'Report back to me once you're done – and ride safely!' He gave me a threatening wink before poopsnaggling off down the hall to brush teeth.

The tooth bike
(pre-accident)

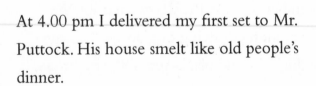

At 4.00 pm I delivered my first set to Mr. Puttock. His house smelt like old people's dinner.

'Oh, lovely. Thank you, boy. And, here, take some money.'

He pressed a 20-cent piece into my hand and closed my fingers around it. 'Buy yourself an ice-cream,' he said.

I forced a smile and pocketed the 20, not having the heart to tell him what year it was.

I took off down the hill on my bike, dashing all over town, top speed, delivering teeth like they were newspapers. I could get off the bike, knock, deliver and be back onboard faster than a paper dude could chuck the *Echo* onto the lawn. Almost, anyway. That old bike hadn't been so fast in the 90 years since it came off the production line. With the speed I was doing I deserved double pay. Smith would have to make more dentures just to keep up with my deliveries. I was the Lance Armstrong of the tooth delivery world. In two days' time Sasha would be surrounded by large popcorns, slushees and choc tops. And, at top speed, I think the bike looked less pink. It almost looked red.

But even at that electrifying pace I found myself with just 15 minutes left and 12 sets undelivered. I calculated that I had one minute and 15 seconds to deliver each set of teeth. Easy. I took a shortcut down Compton Lane and whipped across the empty block. I sped down through the narrow, winding road behind the quarry. I must have been doing 50 kilometres an hour, trailer rattling along happily behind, when something moved at the corner of my eye. A garbage truck was pulling out of the council depot. My cat-like reflexes kicked in and I swerved onto the wrong side of the road. A car was tearing towards me from the opposite direction. I slammed the brakes and shredded a tyre, which made the tooth trailer wobble violently behind. I thought I had it under control but then the trailer flipped, snapping the bar that connected it to the bike. I stopped but the trailer kept screaming down the road, shooting sparks and rolling directly towards the garbage truck that was pulling out in front of me. The truck driver saw it at the last second before impact. The trailer slammed into a silver drum on the side of his truck, burst open and came to rest beneath the back wheels.

'Watch where you're goin', you goose,' yelled the tattooed driver with missing front teeth as he looked down to see if there was any damage. I jumped off the bike, dumped it beside the road and ran towards the trailer but, before I got there, the driver hit the accelerator and drove right over it. He crushed it into the road like a soft-drink can. I looked for the truck's numberplate but it was covered in garbage juice, dripping from the back of the truck.

As the engine noise became a distant groan I walked slowly over to the mangled wreck.

It reminded me of my hopes and dreams of having Sasha fall in love with me. This is what I would look like, too, once Mum heard that I had blown the job.

The trailer doors were open and teeth had leapt from their containers. A few sets had tyre prints across the gums. They were pressed into the bitumen like roadkill. Most were scattered across the road but still okay – top teeth without bottoms, bottoms without tops. It was like a big tooth-and-gum omelette cooking on the road. Flies had already arrived on the scene.

The way I saw it, I had three choices:

1) Tell Mum and Bryce Smith that I screwed up.

2) Bury the teeth and leave town.

3) Lie and –

My mobile rang. I ripped it out of my pocket, staring at the screen. 5.19 pm. This would be Smith, checking in. But I didn't

When False teeth escape

ha ha Ha Ha
ha ha hA ha

want it to be him. I thought about throwing
the phone somewhere. Somewhere far, far
away. Like into the quarry. The phone kept
barking. I couldn't take it anymore so I
stabbed the green button, but I didn't say
anything.

'Tom?'

I could still hang up or make out like I was
in a bad mobile area.

'Tom?'

Seconds ticked like hours.

'Thomas!'

'Yes!' I said sharply.

'Oh, you are there. How's it going?' said Smith.

'Um . . . good,' I said, looking at the contents of my trailer mashed into the road. A car came round the corner and I stepped aside. It weaved around the accident but squished one random set of teeth.

'You okay?' the driver asked. He was wearing reindeer antlers on his head.

I waved and nodded. The car kept moving.

'What was that?' Bryce asked.

'Nothing,' I said, an idea coming to me. 'It was nothing. Look, I might be a little late. Could you give me till six?'

'Indeedley doodley,' said Smith. 'I've got tools to polish. But no later. We don't want to be awake when Santa Claus arrives, do we?'

I pressed 'End' and leaned down, grabbing an empty case. Then I did the only thing I could do, the only thing that would allow me to get paid, stay alive until Boxing Day and

show Sasha what a guy I was. I paired up sets
of teeth and jammed them together. I didn't
know which tops went with which bottoms,
but I didn't have time for petty details. I
slipped teeth into containers and stuffed them
into my pockets. I dragged the trailer off the
road, dumped it behind a hedge and jumped
onto Pinky, the one-tyred bike.

Here comes Santa Claus. Here comes Santa Claus.
That was the song running through my head
as I pedalled. Next stop: J. Larstead.

'Thank you, dear,' she said. 'Merry
Christmas.'

'Um, would you mind just trying them on
for me?' I asked.

She looked at me a little funny but opened
the container and shoved the toppies in.

'Well, they feel a wee bit big,' she said.

'Right,' I said, pulling another slightly

cracked container out of my pocket. 'Well, try these.'

She frowned as she attempted to push the new set in.

'No, they feel a bit small.'

After just three or four sets we had a pair that almost matched.

'Merry Christmas!' I called as I bolted across the lawn, wiping the old lady's spit off the teeth she'd tried.

I checked my list and headed off to my next address.

Next day, Christmas, Smith showed up at our house around nine. I was in the garage desperately trying to beat the trailer back into shape. When I heard him arrive I threw an old paint sheet over it and ran inside. My mum was kissing him. And this was no peck on the cheek.

When they were done he handed me a small present. I ripped open the wrapping. It was a watch, a super-nice one.

'Thanks,' I said. I took it into the lounge room. Mum headed for the kitchen to fix Bryce a drink, and he came and sat next to me on the couch.

'How do you like it? Look, it's just like mine.' He showed me his wrist with the exact same watch.

'It's awesome,' I said. I was just about to ask him when he might pay me for yesterday's work when he looked around and lowered his voice. 'Listen, I had a call from a patient last night. She said that she had found some small pieces of gravel in her teeth. You don't know anything about that, do you?'

I kept my eyes firmly on the watch and shook my head. 'No, who was it?'

'Jean Larstead.'

Adrenaline shot through me but I kept cool. 'Nope. I dunno.'

'Oh, well, never mind. Some of these oldies are just looking for an excuse to complain. She probably just imagined it, the old coot.' He laughed. 'But listen, you'll have to deliver the bike and trailer back to the surgery bright and early on the 27th. Or, actually, I could just take it with me today. I'll put it in the back of the wagon.'

'No, it's okay,' I said quickly. 'I'll bring it back. It's kind of fun, riding around with a trailer. '

Later, as we sat down to Christmas lunch, Bryce's phone beeped.

'Excuse me,' he said as he read the message. 'What in heaven's name?'

'Are you okay?' Mum asked.

'One of the patients says that his dentures taste like garbage.'

'How odd,' said my mum.

'Do you know anything about this, Tom?'
he asked.

My mother glared. I shook my head.

I kept quiet as we jammed ourselves with
chicken and pavlova. Then Bryce wanted to
play table tennis in the garage. I said no but he
insisted. I tried to keep him and Mum down
the roller-door end, away from the covered-up
trailer. I won the first game 21–12. Halfway
through the second, Bryce's phone rang. He
groaned.

'My apologies, you'll have to excuse me
again. For some silly reason I agreed to be on
call today.'

My heart missed a beat.

He took the call, wandering around the
garage, saying, 'I see,' a lot.

I stood there, nervously gnawing on the
rubber bit of my table tennis bat.

When the call was over he said, 'One of
the patients that you delivered to yesterday

claims to have tyre tracks on his teeth and gums. That's the third complaint I've received. Are you certain that you don't know anything about this, Thomas?'

I shook my head. My mother started massaging her temples.

'There wasn't an accident of any kind, was there? You didn't drop any of the teeth?'

I shook my head again, but only very slightly.

Bryce narrowed his eyes. My mother clicked her tongue. It was like being in a police line-up, but I was the only suspect.

'Tom?' my mother said, almost whispering, knowing that I'd done something wrong.

'Well . . .' I said, taking a deep breath. 'There was a little problem with the trailer.'

I turned to the paint sheet with the trailer underneath. I looked at it for a moment, trying to think of a way out of this. But I was in too deep now. I reached down and slowly pulled the cover off, revealing the trailer in all its twisted glory.

'You little liar! Give me that watch,' Bryce said.

'Hang on a minute. Don't you call my son a liar.'

'I just did. He has been totally irresponsible and then lied about it!'

'Well, let's talk to him about it and find a solution,' Mum said.

'A solution? The solution is that the boy needs a hiding. It's clear that there's no discipline in this house.'

'Excuse me?' she said.

Uh-oh. That was exactly what you didn't say to my mum. This was going to get ugly.

I started backing up. I slipped quietly out of the garage and into the house. As I tiptoed down the hall I could hear them shouting. Mum was giving it to him, really standing up for me. Go Mum. I slipped out the back door, grabbed my bike and clipped my helmet. I jumped on and rode down the side of the house, across the lawn and safely out onto the road to Jack's place.

I ate a second Christmas lunch at Jack's. I hadn't heard from Mum. When we were eating dessert – cheesecake with berries – I asked Mrs Danalis, Jack's mum, if she would adopt me, as a Christmas present.

She said no.

Later that afternoon we were playing classic catches on the front lawn and my mum pulled up out front, ordering me into the car.

'You're grounded for the rest of your life,' she said as we drove off.

'Even when I'm 35?' I asked.

'Even when you're 35.'

'Even when I'm 70?'

'Even when you're 70.'

I tried to stay quiet and act like I was ashamed of what I'd done, but I couldn't help myself. There was something I needed to know. 'Can I ask you something?'

'Yes,' she said through gritted teeth.

'Do you think Bryce will still pay me for yesterday?'

TOP SECRET!

Girl I like most in my class

- ~~CHARLOTTE~~
- ~~Sophie~~ (she's CRAZY!)
- ~~Isabella~~ 💗
- ~~Lily~~ (really funny!) → BUT NOT IN A GOOD WAY.
- ~~CHARLOTTE~~
- ~~Isabella~~ (never. again!)
- ~~Veronica~~

- ~~Isabella~~

→ **SASHA!**

Soap

I came up with an ingenious way of making sure I don't mix things up in the shower:

BUM --- fAce

my soap idea

Hover Everything

7 am. My alarm clock goes off. I fling an arm over and knock it off my bedside table. But when the clock falls off the table I don't hear a *bang*. This is weird. Usually it smashes to the floor and Mum yells at me from the kitchen. I always hear a *bang*. Today, I don't hear a thing.

I open one eye, roll over and look down beside my bed. The clock looks like it's floating about 20 centimetres above the floor. I sit up, swing my legs over the side of the bed and stand.

Something else is weird. My feet aren't touching the ground. I am hovering. It feels like I'm standing on a very firm, invisible mattress or a sheet of slightly spongy glass.

I look around my room. It's pretty dark, only lit by the sun squeezing through the cracks at the edge of the blinds, but I can see that my bed is hovering. So is my chest of drawers, my rug and my wardrobe. Three pairs of undies that have been lying on my floor for a week are hovering above the ground. A mouldy sandwich that I threw at the bin yesterday afternoon
is hovering.
So is the bin.

Suddenly
I get it. I'm
dreaming. But
I don't want to
wake up. This is
so much cooler
than most of
my dreams. So I

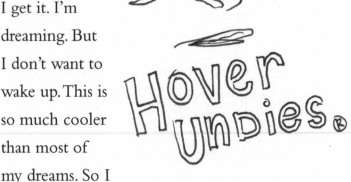

Hover Undies.®

pretend not to know that it's a dream.

I hover-walk over to my bedroom door, looking down at my feet as I go. It's like there's an invisible force field between me and the floor. I open my door and step into the hall. I can't smell toast or coffee, but I can hear something weird in the lounge room.

My soccer ball is hovering in the hall. I kick it softly and it hover-bounces up towards the front door. I grin. I walk into the lounge room. I stop dead in my tracks. The couch is hovering. So is the coffee table, the lamp and the bookcase.

My mum is sitting on the couch. Actually, she's floating slightly above it. She is listening to Pop's old battery-powered radio. She must have dug it out of the shed.

'What's going on?' I say.

'Sssshhhhh!' She turns the volume up.

A news reporter says, 'Scientists around the globe are baffled. Some suggest that there has been a rush of negative electrons from the earth into the objects around us, causing electromagnetic repulsion. A leading European scientist posits that a massive, random superstring has wrapped itself around the earth and caused a local distortion of the fabric of space and time. While environmentalists point the finger at global warming.'

Mum turns a dial to another station. 'In Afghanistan's capital, Kabul,' says another reporter, 'bombs are simply refusing to land. The –'

Mum switches off the radio and drops it onto the couch. It hovers. I laugh. She looks at me. She doesn't think that this is as cool as I do.

I pour dog food into Bando's hoverbowl. The food floats in the air above the bowl in little, meaty hoverballs.

'Bando, breakfast!'

He is up the back in the corner of the yard near the passionfruit vine, crouched, doing a poo. As he hovers away from it he turns and sees that it's floating and he freaks out. He barks at it like it's coming to get him.

'Bando! Stop barking. It's okay, dude. It's just . . . hoverpoo.'

Bando bolts across the yard, up the steps and into the house, top speed.

I follow him up the steps, picking my undies out of my bottom as I go. I think I have my first hoverwedgie.

hoverpoo
(enough said.)

I can't make toast because there's no electricity for some reason. I try to make cereal. The milk hangs over the bowl in marble-sized blobs and the Sultana Bran floats all around it. I put down my spoon and suck up the blobs. I try brushing my hair but I can't get the brush close to my head and my hair keeps sticking straight up.

'I'm going,' I say, grabbing my bag from near the front door.

Mum's in the dining room talking on the phone. 'Could you hold on for a moment?' she says into the phone. Then she calls, 'Tom, school might not be on.'

'It will be,' I say.

'It might not be. I don't want you –'

'I'll come home if it's not.'

'Tom!' she says, getting annoyed. 'This is –'

'I don't want to interrupt your call,' I say. 'Seeya.'

I disappear out the front door.

Outside, I see the old guy who dresses all in white, walking his small black hoverdog.

After he goes by, a cat jumps out of the maple tree on the other side of the street, but it doesn't land. It hovers, which totally weirds the cat out. It looks around and down at its feet, then it screeches loudly and runs in three quick circles, chasing its tail before disappearing into a hedge.

The only things that still seem to be connected to the ground are the road, the trees, the telegraph poles and the houses. Anything not absolutely rooted to the ground is up. Even our car hovers in the driveway.

'Woooooooo!' A Year Three kid from school rides past on his hoverbike, screaming. I think about getting my own bike out of the shed, but then I see the best thing that I have ever seen.

My skateboard.

It's lying on the edge of the driveway, upside down. It is hovering. I walk towards it and flip it up the right way. It still hovers. I jump on. It feels good. I put my left foot down and push through the air. I glide. I push again. I glide down the driveway. I'm in heaven. It's like regular skating but smoother, lighter. I'm skating on air. I turn and push again, heading out across the grass.

'Mum, look!' She peers through the lounge room window. 'A hoverboard!'

She's still on the phone. She tries to smile but I can tell that she is worried about the whole hover thing. She worries way too much. Me? I never worry. This is going to be the best day of my life.

I cane across the grass, hit the edge of the driveway, jump and fall flat on my back. I look up at the sky and wait for the pain, but it doesn't come. I feel a stab of fear that this might still be a dream. But, somehow, I know that it's not.

I glide through the school gates and kick up my board. Kids are bouncing basketballs that don't hit the ground. Girls hoverskip. And I notice that everything is slightly higher than when I first woke up. I feel like I'm maybe 50 centimetres off the ground now rather than 20.

When the bell rings we head to morning lines. Only about half the kids are there. Someone near me starts laughing. I look up to see our hoverprincipal, Mr Ward, coming down the stairs of the main building. His tie is hovering way up over his shoulder. He grabs it and tucks it into his pants, but it untucks straightaway and hovers again. There are giggles. His long moustache hovers slightly at the ends, too. He looks a bit like a circus ringmaster. But the thing that really gets us is that his toupee, a little round wig that covers his bald patch, is hovering. And I don't think he knows. Maybe the teachers were too scared

hoverprincipal
just like the real thing, only a whole lot funnier.

to tell him. He clears
his throat and claps a little
rhythm. We clap back. We try
to be quiet but there are snorts of laughter all
around.

'Thank you, everybody,' he says. 'I realise
that this is a somewhat … unusual day, but I
expect that everybody will be paying attention
to their teachers and focusing on their regular
lessons while we wait for this … phenomenon
to wear off or …' He is lost for words. He
grabs his tie and holds it down. Jack points

at the hoverwig and Mr Ward sees him. The principal reaches up to his floating rug and grabs it. He shoves it into his pocket. Everyone goes wild, laughing. We can't help it. Mr Ward looks like he's about to explode, but there are too many of us to put on detention.

'That will be all,' he says, barely containing his rage. He turns and hovers back up the stairs, one hand covering his bald spot.

I tip orange cordial out of my drink bottle onto the floor but it hovers in little orange blobs around my shoes.

'Very interesting,' Miss Norrish, our teacher, says. She has asked us each to make a short presentation exploring some aspect of the hover thing.

I bend down and flick one of the blobs and it breaks into about 17 smaller splodges.

'So, Tom, what would be your explanation

for the way the liquid is behaving?'

'Well …' I have no idea but I make up something and we discuss the possibilities for a while. Jack is the next to give his presentation.

'Okay, Jack, what are you presenting today?'

'Hovernits!' he says.

'I'm sorry?' Miss Norrish says.

'If you look carefully, my nits are hovering!'

A few kids laugh. Sasha points to Jack's hair and says, 'OMG, they are!'

It's true. My best friend has hovernits. His hair is sticking up like everyone else's, but then there's a thick brown halo of nits hovering above that. It's like space junk in orbit around the earth. Everybody cracks up. Including Jack. When the bell rings for

JACK has hovernits orbiting his HeaD.

recess we bolt outside. Everything is hovering a bit higher. We're probably a metre off the ground now.

I have a chocolate yoghurt in my lunchbox. When I peel back the lid the choc goo flies out of the container and spatters my face. Jack thinks it's the funniest thing he's ever seen. We spend recess jumping out of a tree over near the bubblers. No matter how far we fall we never get hurt.

It seriously is the best day of school ever. Nothing is normal or regular or dull. And as things hover higher and higher it's even more fun. By lunchtime we're about three metres off the ground. We have to do afternoon lessons in the playground because our desks and chairs are right up near the classroom ceiling.

When the bell rings for the end of school everything is at least ten metres off the ground. We're way up above the buildings. Mum is waiting for me, hovering above the main school gate. The parents all look totally spooked.

'What are you doing here?' I ask.

'We've got to rescue your nan,' she says.

'Why?'

'Why? Because I've been at work all day and she's clutching the top of a tree in her front yard, that's why.'

'Oh.'

Mum's voice sounds shaky.

'It's okay, Mum.'

'No, it's not okay, Tom. What do you think is going to happen if everything suddenly falls? Have you thought about that? Or what if we just keep getting higher?'

I try to keep up with Mum as she walks and I think about what she said. She sure has a way of making fun stuff seem not that fun. I look down at the ground and the houses way below me. I feel like I'm walking across a glass-bottom bridge. If we fall right now we'll be mashed into the footpath. Or what if we keep going up? How high can we go? Skyscraper high? Space? The moon? I laugh. Mum frowns. I stop.

Nan's place is down near the beach. I can see the tips of the tallest pine trees on the beachfront. There are heaps of people way up in the trees, sitting on branches. Not just kids but whole families with sleeping bags and everything. In case everything falls, I guess.

We arrive at Nan's. She's in her own tree.

'You took your sweet time getting here,' she calls. 'I've been up this thing for two hours.'

'C'mon, down you come, you silly old thing,' Mum says. She slowly coaxes her down out of the tree. Nan's skirt is hovering up in the air and I can see her giant old-lady undies. I try to turn away but I can't stop looking. I'm going to be scarred for life. Nan tries to pull her skirt down but it hovers over her head again.

'That's something I bet you never thought you'd see,' she says, giving me a wink. 'At least I put my nice undies on.'

We head down the hill towards the beach. The waves are big. Like, massive. That's when I see the weirdest thing I've seen on the weirdest day of my life. There's a thick black and silvery layer hovering ten metres above the water. Fish. Thousands of them. Millions maybe. And sharks and eels. Some are still moving but most aren't. For some reason the ocean isn't hovering, just the animals. Fishermen are out walking through the blanket of fish, sweeping them up in their nets. It sure makes their job easier but seeing all those fish just floating there, dead, makes me feel really sad.

11.30 pm. I'm staring up at the night sky.

We're camped out above our backyard. Just

me, Mum, Nan and my sister Tanya, sleeping under the stars. But I can't sleep. I roll over and look out across town. We are about 40 metres above the ground. Nearly half a football field high. The street lights are off. It's a full moon. There is a patchy blanket of mashed potatoey cloud not far above our heads. It feels like I could almost touch it. The houses and cars, our whole neighbourhood, just hangs there like a thousand flying saucers waiting to crash land.

Nobody has any definite answers. Everything, all over the globe, has hovered for an entire day and nobody knows why.

Some people around town are wearing parachutes. Others are sleeping on piles of mattresses to give them padding if things come crashing down. Only the tips of three or four trees are still above the hoverzone and there have been near-riots with people fighting for space in the trees. Four doors up from our place there's an old inventor guy with a really messy yard. He's sleeping on the bonnet of a rusted car, wearing a homemade jet pack. I hope it works.

I hear Mum's voice.

'You okay?'

'Yeah.'

'You're not scared are you?'

'Nah,' I lie.

'We'll be okay,' she says, but I know she doesn't believe it. She thinks we'll all be smashed into a million little pieces in the morning.

'I love you.'

'You too.'

I close my eyes and wish that everything would stop hovering, that everything would go back to being boring and normal.

I don't really remember much after that. It feels like I fall into a deep sleep that I might never wake up from.

7 am. My alarm clock goes off. I fling an arm over and knock it off my bedside table.

BANG!

My eyes snap open.

'Tom, you'll break that clock one of these days,' says a muffled voice from the kitchen.

I sit up and look around my room. *Why am I in bed?* is the first question that enters my mind. I swing my legs over the side of the bed and gently put my feet down. They touch floorboards. I stand and look around at my wardrobe and bookcase, my mouldy sandwich, my three pairs of undies. They're all sitting on the ground, just like they used to.

Suddenly I get it. I'm dreaming. Otherwise I'd be in my backyard with a thousand broken bones. And all the furniture in my room could not crash from the ceiling to the floor in the night without getting broken and without

187

even waking me. No way. I'm dreaming. But I don't want to wake up. I like this. If I wake up now I'll only be waking into hoverlife, which is a nightmare. So I pretend not to know that it's a dream.

I walk slowly, carefully, over to the window. I get ready to pull the blind, frightened of what I'll see.

'One …' I whisper to myself. 'Two …' I take a deep breath. 'Three.' I pull the long white cord, revealing the world outside.

Green grass. Our street. Birds tweeting. My regular junk on the lawn. Nothing is a mess. The cars aren't smashed to pieces. Everything is perfect.

I run to my bedroom door.

'Mum!'

I swing the door open. The smell of coffee and toast. I walk into the lounge room. The couch isn't hovering. Neither is the coffee table, lamp or rug.

Mum is in the kitchen buttering toast. Regular toast. Not hovertoast.

'Why's everything down?' I ask.

'Huh?' she says, putting the butter in the fridge and crossing back to the bench.

'Why isn't everything hovering?'

Mum turns and looks at me, blank-faced. 'I don't know what you're talking about Tom, and I'm late. What do you want, Vegemite or honey?' she says.

'Um . . . honey,' I say. I can't believe this. She honestly seems to not know what I'm talking about.

I go out the back to look around. Everything looks like it always does. Everything looks . . . kind of dull.

But then I see something. Bando is up in the corner of the yard near the passionfruit vine, doing what he does every morning, like clockwork. When he finishes, he turns quickly and looks at what he's done. He growls at it.

Then he backs up and runs into the house, top speed.

And that's how I know that it happened.

Bando knows.

Everything hovered. Just for one day. It really did.

hover everything

Acknowledgements

Thanks to Paul Jennings for writing the wonderful short stories that I grew up on.

Thanks to Edensor Park Public School. kids for brainstorming Tough Nana ideas with me at BookFeast 2010. And to the students at Wallacia, Mulgoa, Glenmore Park, Regentville, Surveyors Creek, Nicholson Street, Lightning Ridge, Collinsville, Scottville and St John Bosco schools for brainstorming NanFight and Hover Everything ideas with me. Cheers to the Byron Young Writers' Boot Camp, too. Thanks to Finnian O'Connor for his annoying ideas. I had fascinating Hover Science discussions with Mike Mansted, Shave, Charlton Hill, Michael Pryor and Dr Karl. Thanks to Sophie Hamley, Zoe Walton and Brandon VanOver for being my teachers and for encouraging my creative endeavours, no matter how weird or gross they may be. Cheers to Gusto Gordon for making Tom complete. Thanks to Amb, Hux and Luca for being funny, imaginative and keeping me on my toes. But, mostly, thanks to Joey 'Jaws' Chestnut for eating 68 hot dogs in ten minutes. You're an inspiration to us all.

Tristan Bancks is a children's and teen author with a background in acting and filmmaking. His books include the *My Life* series, *Mac Slater* (Australia and US) and *Two Wolves* (*On the Run* in the US), a crime-mystery novel for middle-graders. *Two Wolves* won Honour Book in the 2015 Children's Book Council of Australia Book of the Year Awards and was shortlisted for the Prime Minister's Literary Awards. It also won the YABBA and KOALA Children's Choice Awards. His new novel, *The Fall*, is available from May 2017. Tristan is a writer–ambassador for the literacy charity Room to Read. He is excited by the future of storytelling and inspiring others to create.

Gus Gordon has written and illustrated over 70 books for children. He writes books about motorbike-riding stunt chickens, dogs that live in trees, and singing on rooftops in New York. His picture book *Herman and Rosie* was a 2013 CBCA Honour Book. Gus loves speaking to kids about illustration, character design and the desire to control a wiggly line. Visit Gus at www.gusgordon.com

MY LIFE AND OTHER STUFF THAT WENT WRONG

Is your grandpa super-angry? Has your nan ever tried to climb Mt Everest? Have you started your own playground freak show? And have you ever risked your life to save your pet rat from certain destruction?

I have. I'm Tom Weekly and this is my life. Inside the covers of this book you'll read lots of weird-funny-gross stories and learn the secret of my strangest body part. But I guarantee that won't freak you out as much as the story of how Stella Holling, a girl who's been in love with me since second grade, tricked me into kissing her.

Available now

MY LIFE AND OTHER MASSIVE MISTAKES

Have you ever helped your pop escape from a nursing home? Does your teacher have a problem with his bowels? Is your sister an evil genius and criminal mastermind? Have you ever mined your teeth for cash? Do you want to know where all the lost socks go? Is there a girl or boy at school who's desperate to kiss you? And do you know someone with the worst case of nits in world history?

I do. I'm Tom Weekly and this is the third book in my weird, funny, sometimes gross life story.

Available now

TWO WOLVES

'Gripping and unpredictable, with a hero you won't forget.' – John Boyne, author of *The Boy in the Striped Pyjamas*

One afternoon, police officers show up at Ben Silver's front door. Minutes after they leave, his parents arrive home. Ben and his little sister Olive are bundled into the car and told they're going on a holiday. But are they?

It doesn't take long for Ben to realise that his parents are in trouble. Ben's always dreamt of becoming a detective – his dad even calls him 'Cop'. Now Ben gathers evidence and tries to uncover what his parents have done.

The problem is, if he figures it out, what does he do? Tell someone? Or keep the secret and live life on the run?

Available now

About Tristan Bancks and Room to Read

Tristan Bancks is a committed writer–ambassador for Room to Read, an innovative global non-profit that has impacted the lives of over ten million children in ten low-income countries through its Literacy and Girls' Education programs. Room to Read is changing children's lives in Bangladesh, Cambodia, India, Laos, Nepal, South Africa, Sri Lanka, Tanzania, Vietnam and Zambia – and you can help!

In 2012 Tristan started the Room to Read World Change Challenge in collaboration with Australian school children to build a school library in Siem Reap, Cambodia. Over the years since Tristan, his fellow writer–ambassadors and kids in both Australia and Hong Kong have raised $80,000 to buy 80,000 books for children in low-income countries.

For more information or to join this year's World Change Challenge, visit http://www.tristanbancks.com/p/change-world.html, and to find out more about Room to Read, visit www.roomtoread.org.